Whiteout

A sort of numbness settled in Rob's mind, matching the numbness of his face and hands and feet. His eyes ached from straining through wind and driving snow, but all he could see was a mass of greyish whirling dots. Suddenly all the familiar landmarks were gone, obliterated in a blanket of white...

Just in time, Amos the shepherd rescues Rob from the deadly freezing whiteout. But the storm continues, leaving deep snowdrifts all around. Soon they are prisoners in Amos's lonely hillside home.

Over the next few days an unlikely friendship develops—the boy helps the ailing old man tend his sheep and Amos proves to be a good listener. For the first time Rob talks about a guilty secret and discovers that things aren't as bad as he'd thought.

And at night, Rob dreams—vivid dreams of the distant past—about strangers with problems very different from his own who find a remarkably similar answer.

Past and present are woven together in this unusual adventure.

Eleanor Watkins lives in the hills where Rob's adventure takes place. She has written many short stories for magazines and twelve books for children. Her historical children's adventure, *Greyback* is also published by Lion.

Whiteout

Eleanor Watkins

A LION BOOK

Copyright © 1994 Eleanor Watkins

The author asserts the moral right
to be identified as the author of this work

Published by
Lion Publishing plc
Sandy Lane West, Oxford, England
ISBN 0 7459 2768 8
Albatross Books Pty Ltd
PO Box 320, Sutherland, NSW 2232, Australia
ISBN 0 7324 0810 5

First edition 1994

All rights reserved

A catalogue record for this book is available
from the British Library

Printed and bound in Great Britain
by Cox & Wyman Ltd, Reading

Contents

1	The Quad	7
2	Old Amos	14
3	The Dream	26
4	Cuckoo Time	31
5	Secret Valley	37
6	Lamb?	45
7	The Raid	51
8	Blizzard	56
9	Twins	64
10	Time to Leave	68
11	The Great Spirit	73
12	The Cave	79
13	Wolves	84
14	No sign of life	90
15	Hope	95
16	Rescue?	101
17	Sacrifice	107
18	HELP	117
19	Rob's secret	123
20	The Sea King	133
21	Together again	138
	Postscript	150

1
The Quad

The wind stung his face with freezing sleet as Clive Roberts got off the school bus. He hunched his shoulders and took a tighter grip of his sports bag, heading into the wind. No familiar Land Rover waited for him at the corner today. It would be a long cold walk home.

He walked with his mates for a while, then they turned off as they reached their own gates or roads or short cuts between the houses.

'Bye, Rob!'

'See ya!'

'Don't forget rugby practice tomorrow, Rob!'

Then the last estate on the edge of the small town was left behind, and Rob was on his own, facing a lonely uphill walk between bare hedges and windswept fields.

The sleet was turning to snow now, beginning to stick on the hazel and bramble twigs along the hedgerow. His hands were red with cold already, because as always he had resisted his mother's suggestion of gloves and scarf that morning. Things like that were definitely 'uncool' now that he was thirteen. Mum was always a bit fussy, and perhaps a little more edgy than usual that morning because of the long trip to London and the sadness of the funeral service ahead of her. She didn't like not being there when he got in from school, and he wasn't too keen on the idea himself. It gave him a bleak kind of feeling in his middle that was partly hunger but not altogether.

The landmarks passed. The sharp right fork in the road, the narrow steep-verged bend where you hoped not to meet something coming the other way, the little holiday cottage beside the road, the long pull up the hill. Finally, the first glimpse of home, the farmhouse between its sheltering oaks and sycamores, as he turned into the drive between Dad's fields of winter barley and oil-seed rape.

The house looked sad and lonely. There was no smoke rising from the sitting-room chimney, the sheepdog Gem was chained to her kennel, there was no car, and the Land Rover was neatly garaged. Rob freed Gem who, pleased to see him, leaped high in the air to lick his face. He gave her the remains of a Mars bar in his pocket, found the key on a high shelf in the garage and let himself in.

There was no welcoming smell of cooking, but a meal on a plate in the fridge, which he heated in the microwave and ate on a chair pulled close to the Aga, thawing his feet against its warm front. A couple of slices of fruit cake followed. Rob dumped the plates in the sink and idly switched on the answering machine

Dad had installed to deal with calls from the corn merchants, which always seemed to come when both he and Mum were out of doors together. There was only one message—his brother Peter's voice, brief and to the point. 'I won't be home until about ten. Got an extra trip. You'll have to look at the ewes. And don't eat my dinner as well as your own!'

Rob grinned, flicking off the switch. That sounded like his brother! Pete had his HGV licence, and did long-distance trips to interesting-sounding places. He started in the early hours and was usually home by four-thirty in the afternoon, unless it was a night-out trip. Dad had depended on him to look at the in-lamb ewes this evening and Mum to keep an eye on Rob. Now it was all down to Rob himself.

But there were advantages to being alone for a while. Changing into his jeans and sweater, Rob took a prowl round the forbidden territory of Pete's room, seeing what new CDs he had and twiddling the knobs of the player. He even opened Pete's wardrobe and tried on his motorcycling jacket and helmet, which was too big and came down over his eyes. Pete's room was pleasantly muddled and untidy, but nothing like as messy as his own.

By contrast, the bedroom next door belonging to his second brother Nick was pin-neat and spotless when he opened the door. Mum had cleaned and tidied everything when Nick left, duvet uncreased, books in neat rows on the shelves, records stacked. A row of Airfix model planes and tanks were neatly laid out on the chest of drawers. Rob walked over and turned the propeller of one, with a great sense of daring. It would be more than his life was worth to touch those models if Nick had been home. But of course he wasn't, and hadn't been for months, and wouldn't be for a long time yet. Perhaps never...

But that train of thought only brought the familiar, horrid, sick feeling to his stomach. He put down the model quickly and closed the door of Nick's room behind him.

Downstairs again, he decided against switching on the TV. It might be one of those news programmes again, and he avoided them when he could.

Besides, there were the sheep to be seen to.

It was snowing properly now, wet cold flakes that were sticking and covering the ground with a soft feathery layer of white. The in-lamb ewes were still out in the field next to the farm buildings, ready to come in for their confinements. The first lambs were not due until the beginning of March, more than a week away, but there were always one or two early ones to look out for. Rob heaved a sigh, pulling on his boots. He didn't like farm work at all, much, and he especially disliked anything to do with sheep. Stupid, brainless creatures! Give him something mechanical any day.

But there was nothing else for it. With Gem at his heels, he took the bucket of sheep-nuts out to the field and tipped it into the trough, counting the mass of bleating and shoving woolly bodies. He knew there should be fifty-three, but at the first try counted only fifty-one. The second go yielded fifty-two, but try as he might he could not account for the fifty-third. They were definitely one short.

Rob frowned, stuffing his hands into the pockets of his jacket and scanning the hedgerows. The sheep had the run of two fields, the near one by the farm buildings and an adjoining steep banky field rising to a high point on the hillside. No sign of any movement, indeed the landscape was blurred and greyish with falling snow. He would have to search, though. The missing ewe could very likely be lambing in some hidden corner. It would be a long trek.

Then he remembered the Quad, the useful four-wheeled all-terrain vehicle used by Dad and Pete on such occasions. He was still considered too young to ride it himself, to his great disgust. But he'd had a few tries on the quiet, when Mum was safely out of the way, and felt quite confident of handling it. It was just what he needed now to find the sheep.

He left Gem shut up in the feed store with a handful of dog biscuits. She was old and arthritic and it wouldn't be fair to make her keep up with the Quad. It started first go, and Rob rode it through the gate and into the field, sliding and skidding a little in the slippery snow. He had remembered a helmet but forgotten gloves, and his hands were soon chilled and raw again. He went round the field where the sheep were, peering into hedgerows and behind bushes. No sign of the missing ewe, and darkness was beginning to fall. Rob put the vehicle into top gear and headed for the steep field.

Snow was falling thickly now, and it was getting

harder to see ahead. The Quad's wheels gripped and skidded and gripped again, pulling steadily. Rob began to feel a powerful sense of achievement. For once he was in charge, managing the Quad in spite of treacherous conditions, taking responsibility, no longer the helpless baby of the family.

No sign of any sheep, though. Then, right at the top of the bank, where the field opened into a deep sunken lane leading to the open mountain, a small hole showed in the hedge beside the gate, and, caught in the hawthorn twigs, a scrap of sheep's wool. Rob stared at it, idling the Quad's engine. He'd seen enough of sheep to know that the small hole was quite big enough for a ewe, intent on escape, to squeeze through. Had it not been feeding time, the whole lot would probably have followed.

He hesitated, his bare knuckles wet and hurting with cold and his feet freezing. There was a wet numb patch on one knee where he had a hole in his jeans. The warm kitchen at home beckoned strongly for a moment. But there was only one thing to do and he knew it. He opened the gate and rode through, dismounting to close it behind him.

The sunken lane was sheltered from the worst of the wind and snow, but once out on the open mountain his breath was snatched away by the ferocity of the cold strong wind. It tore at him from all directions, spattering snow in his face, buffeting him and his machine. He saw at once that the snow was much thicker here. Already the short turf was covered and last year's bracken fronds stood up in white-covered mounds. Looking back, he could see that the Quad's tracks were filling in almost as quickly as he made them.

The expanse of the mountain spread before him, the steep sides of the Bluff obscured by whirling flakes. He weighed up the situation, the absurdity of trying to find one stray ewe in this whiteout striking him suddenly.

Dad would come and find the sheep in daylight tomorrow.

It probably wasn't lambing in any case, just sheltering quite safely in a ditch somewhere.

Mum wouldn't want him to be out here alone, and he wouldn't get any credit whatever happened, just a lot of hassle.

He hated sheep anyway.

He might as well go home.

Instead, he switched on the headlights on the Quad and began to circle the rough ground. As he peered ahead into the beam of light all he could see was greyish whirling dots.

2

Old Amos

Rob had no idea how much time passed while he searched. A sort of numbness settled in his mind, matching the numbness of his face and hands and feet. His eyes ached from straining through wind and driving snow, but there was no sign of the missing sheep. Once a hare appeared, sitting for a moment staring into the headlights before bounding into the snow in a series of high leaps. But there was nothing else.

Even in the dark Rob could find his way around the lower foothill, knew where the narrow steep sheep-tracks criss-crossed the mountain road, or where a track turned off to one of the remote farms. But suddenly the familiar landmarks were gone, obliterated in a blanket of white. He realized with a sudden shock that he could not even remember which way to go to get back to their own land.

And then the headlights flickered and the engine stuttered. The Quad came to a halt. It had run out of petrol.

Rob dismounted stiffly, his feet and legs feeling as though they did not quite belong. He was suddenly unbearably weary. This hadn't been such a good idea after all. He would have to abandon the Quad and walk home, and it would be a very long walk.

Without the headlights it was now completely dark, with just a faint lightness coming from the snow. He had only the vaguest idea of his whereabouts, but he figured that if he kept heading downhill he would hit familiar ground sooner or later. He put his frozen hands into his pockets and began to walk.

But the entrance to the sunken lane wasn't where he thought it would be. Instead, he floundered over the top of a ridge and into a ditch. He had no idea what ditch it was, or where he should go from there. A great heaviness seized him as he sprawled for a moment in the snow, winded. It was all his own fault. He'd been stupid to come out alone in these conditions. He supposed he might die of exposure out here alone.

He thought about dying for a moment, still sitting in the snow and getting back his breath.

What would it feel like to die?

Would it take long?

Should he pray?

He considered those things, while the snow settled on the helmet he still wore. He'd believed in God since he was small. Now he wasn't quite so sure. He'd prayed to God about Nick, but God hadn't heard. Or at any rate, hadn't answered. It wasn't much good praying now. Much easier just to give up. God would take care of him if he died. But then, he didn't believe in God any more. Or did he?

It would be the ones left behind who suffered most. Mum, Dad, Pete... Nick...

That thought came clearly through increasingly muddled ones. He could not argue with it. He would have to make the effort and find shelter of some kind. He struggled to his feet and began to walk, lifting his feet and pushing them forward mechanically step by step.

To encourage himself, he thought of Mum, stirring something in the warm kitchen at home, and Dad, frowning in concentration over the innards of a tractor. Peter, thumping him none too gently and calling him spaghetti-legs and worse, but always ready to give him 50p when his pocket money ran out. Pete wouldn't have done such a daft thing as take off and get lost in a snowstorm. Pete thought first and acted later, like Dad. Nick might have done the same, though. Rob smiled with stiff lips, remembering Nick's motor-bike taking off from a makeshift ramp over a pile of old tractor tyres and crash-landing on the other side. Nick, still in plaster, getting back on the bike and doing wheelies all round the yard.

His thoughts became confused again. Time was passing—but how fast? How slow? Was he asleep? He felt as thought he was, but he was still on his feet, still moving forward blindly. He'd been thinking about Nick. Suddenly the driving snow became sand, whirling in a frenzy of hot desert air. And then the sun was filtering through from somewhere above, hazy and dim.

He saw that it wasn't the sun at all, but a lighted window. And around the window a solid stone wall. A low building huddled close to the ground against the storm. Outhouses, and the sudden barking of a sheepdog, joined in a moment by another. Then a door opening, and a man's voice speaking and hands pulling him in. Then, for a little while, nothing.

Rob woke up suddenly. There was a fierce painful tingling in all the parts of him that had been numb before, his hands and feet, his nose and his knee where there had been a hole in his jeans. Somehow, his jeans and jacket and boots had been removed, and he'd been wrapped in a rough and rather smelly blanket that scratched and tickled.

He raised his head. He was half-lying on a rickety armchair in a small room lit by yellow light from a hissing paraffin lamp. The room was cluttered and very untidy—a table piled with dirty mugs and plates, old newspapers and empty baked bean cans, and half a stale loaf. An oak dresser with willow-pattern dishes stood against one wall, a narrow bed covered with another rough blanket was against the opposite one, and there was an old stone sink in the corner. A bright fire burned in an old-fashioned range, and a sheepdog lay, nose on paws, in front of it. Beyond it, part of the corner of the room was partitioned off with boards, and something alive rustled inside. An overpowering smell of sheep and dog and paraffin mingled thickly.

Rob wrinkled his nose in distaste, then sneezed. The sound brought an elderly little stick of a man, shrivelled and bent like a blackthorn branch, shuffling up to the armchair where Rob had been deposited. He peered at the boy from shrewd small eyes in a weather-beaten face. He wore a shapeless old pullover and corduroy trousers held up by braces and a belt, and he smelled strongly of sheep. He said, 'Ah, so you be a bit pierter* now, be you?'

Rob guessed that he had passed out for a while. His mouth was dry and his head ached dreadfully. He said, 'Yes, thanks,' and was surprised at the husky croak that came from his throat. He raised himself to sit up, but immediately felt sick as the stuffy room swam before his eyes. The old man reached out a calloused hand to push him back into the chair again.

'You stop quiet there a bit. Dunna try to get up yet. Drink this.'

He held a cracked mug to Rob's lips. Rob swallowed the liquid, which seemed to be warm milk with something added that made him splutter a little. The old man grinned. 'Drop o' brandy. That's what I gives the lambs when they comes in half-starved like you was.'

The drink seemed to settle Rob's stomach and the room stopped spinning. He remembered everything.

He asked weakly, 'Please could I use your phone?'

The old man grinned again, showing discoloured teeth. 'Phone? I hanna got one of them.'

Rob's head began to spin again. He felt suddenly panicky, and felt a strong sense of distaste for the smelly, squalid, strange room, mingled with a desperate longing for home. He said, 'I've got to get in

* livelier, sharper

touch with my Dad and get him to come and fetch me. They've gone off for the day, but they'll be home soon and they won't know where I've gone. They'll be worried.' He wanted to add, 'And I don't like it here. It's strange and it stinks.'

But he repeated instead, 'They'll be worried', and tried not to notice the prickling behind his eyes that felt suspiciously like tears.

The little old man blinked at him. 'Your folks? Where be you from, then?'

'Penvaen. That's a farm, about a mile from—'

The old man interrupted with a nob of his balding head. 'I knows it. Young Jim Roberts' place. You be his boy, then? Well, indeed! You're a long way from home! This is Ty Mynydd, right up over the top. What's your name and what be you doing up here, then?'

He drew up a hard kitchen chair and sat facing Rob, hands on knees. Weakly, Rob explained, about the missing ewe, the Quad, the snowstorm. The old man nodded once or twice, and said, 'Well, you be here for the night, I reckon. No way of getting in touch with your folks before morning. They'll find you all right when daylight comes and it do stop snowing. Very likely get the police and a helicopter out searching when they finds that machine of yours.'

Rob felt a little dazed. He must have travelled much further than he'd thought, and all in the wrong direction. Ty Mynydd was right up under the Bluff, miles from home, tucked away in a fold of the mountains all by itself. This must be old Amos Griffiths. He'd heard his parents speak about him, the last of a long line of sheep-farmers.

'Amos, that's me,' said the old man, echoing his thoughts. 'You'll have to stop here along of me for the night, like it or not. You still looks a bit middlin' to me. Want something to eat?'

The thought of food made Rob feel sick again. The idea of eating anything prepared in this place was revolting anyway. He said, 'No thanks. I had my tea before I started out.'

That seemed a long time ago, almost like another world. An old grandfather clock in the corner pointed to ten past four, but that could not be right. Following his gaze, Amos chuckled wheezily. 'He be stopped for thirty year or more,' he said. He picked up an old-fashioned pocket watch from the dresser and consulted it. 'Five-and-twenty past nine. If I was you, I'd get some sleep. You can have my bed.'

He indicated the blanket-covered bed against the wall. 'I've got beds upstairs but they won't be aired. I mostly sleeps in the warm here, to keep an eye on her and the likes.'

When he sat up a little, Rob could see that the pen in the corner contained a fully-grown ewe, lying in a bed of hay and panting a little. 'Hasn't been quite right for a day or two now. Could lamb any day, so I've been keeping her under my eye and doctoring her up.'

It was no new thing to Rob to have lambs indoors. Dad often brought in lambs that were cold or weak or sickly. They were warmed up in the bottom shelf of the Aga and nursed back to life. But Rob had never seen a full-grown ewe in a living-room before. It explained the strong sheepy smell. He gave a grimace of distaste but was suddenly just too tired to care much about anything. His limbs ached and his eyes were heavy.

'But what about you?' he asked.

'I'll sleep fine in the chair. Got to get up and dose her in the night anyway.' He nodded towards the pen.

Outside the wind whined and the snow blew with a scratching sound against the window. Rob saw that there was no way he was going to get away before the morning. He struggled off the chair and over to the bed, which had rough flannelette sheets under the blankets. The blankets, like everything else, smelled of dog and sheep, and the mattress was lumpy. He thought fleetingly of the well-spring mattress, the crisp clean sheets and bright duvet in his room at home. But it was bliss just to lie down and stretch out his aching limbs.

Rob hoped that he would fall asleep at once, to get the night over as quickly as possible, but for a while sleep seemed to elude him in that strange bed in the strange stuffy room. The old man sat on his hard chair, hands on knees, and after a while his chin sank onto his chest. The sick ewe slept in her pen, panting a little, the sheepdog dozed but kept one ear cocked and one eye half open. The paraffin lamp hissed. A charred log shifted and sent up a shower of sparks. On the mantelpiece above stood a battered tea-caddy, a pot of paper spills and several bottles of sheep medicine.

Rob guessed that the old man's life revolved totally around his sheep—lambing, shearing, dipping, treating for foot rot and maggots and all the diseases peculiar to sheep. Season following season, year after year. He wondered how old Amos was. Great-Uncle Tom in London had been almost eighty when he died. It was difficult to guess a person's age when they were so old.

His thoughts turned back to home and he felt a lump rise in his throat. Were Mum and Dad back from London yet? Had they found he was missing? He turned over under the sheepy-smelling blankets and Amos raised his head to look at him. 'Still awake, then?'

'Yes.'

'Bain't worrying about your folks, be you? Because it's no use doing that. Nothin' more we can do. They're bound to find you in the morning.'

The lump in Rob's throat seemed to grow in size. He tried to say, 'Yes, I know,' but his voice came out as a miserable croak. He knew that the tears were not far away.

Amos was looking at him shrewdly. 'You looks a bit like a lamb that's got parted from its mum, you do. All lost and bewildered-like. Never mind. What do you say to that cup of cocoa now?'

Rob nodded dumbly, the mention of Mum almost making the tears spill over. Pete and Nick sometimes called him a Mummy's boy and maybe he was, just a bit. He wished she was here now, anyway, instead of this inquisitive old man.

Amos picked up a battered old kettle and filled it

from the cold tap at the sink in the corner. He put it to boil over the fire and then went across to the dresser and began to rummage about in one of the cupboards. After a moment he gave a grunt of satisfaction as he found what he was looking for. It was a battered round biscuit tin with a picture of Persian kittens on the lid, which he brought over and placed on the bed beside Rob.

'There. While we're waiting for the kettle, you have a look in there. Full of treasures, that is. My grandsons used to love to have a rummage round in there when they was little, for a treat, when they come to visit me. That'll cheer you up.'

Rob pulled himself up in the bed and took the tin. He wanted to say that he was thirteen years old, not some little kid to be distracted by a collection of odds and ends. But he knew that the old man was only trying to be kind.

The tin was full of out-of-date coins, cigarette cards, unusually fancy buttons and buckles, pencil stubs, medals, brooches and various other bits of bric-a-brac. He rummaged among them half-heartedly, to please the old man, and picked up a greyish stone-like object, small but heavy, shaped to a point at one end.

Amos brought over the mug of hot cocoa and looked at what he had picked out. 'Arrowhead, that is. Used to find them about here, now and again. Bits of carvings on rocks, too. Somebody brought one of 'em into this house when they was building the hearth in the front parlour. You interested in that sort of thing?'

Rob wasn't, particularly. They had been on field trips and visits to old castles and places of archaeological interest once or twice from school, but he had always found it difficult to connect the old artefacts they'd been shown with real people who had actually lived and breathed. He weighed the arrowhead in his hand, putting out a finger to feel its tip. It had worn blunt with age, but maybe once it had been keen and sharp and new. He looked up at Amos. 'Is it hundreds of years old?'

'Hundreds and maybe thousands. I don't know. You've been to school since me. How long ago did folks use arrows around here?'

Dates and times and places had always seemed to elude Rob. Had the 1066 Normans used arrows? Or the Romans? Or was it in the Stone Age? Iron Age? Bronze Age? He blinked and shook his head. 'I don't know,' he said.

'Well, ne' mind. It'll all be the same in another hundred years. Here, drink your cocoa before it gets cold.'

The cocoa was hot and sweet and comforting. Rob felt some of his misery dissolve. It wouldn't be all that long until morning. All he had to do was stick it out.

He picked up the arrowhead for a moment before he lay down again, feeling the cold rough flint grow warm in his hand. The old man had drunk his own cocoa and looked as though he would nod off to sleep at any moment. Outside, the snow scraped the windows with a soft scratchy sound, and the wind was rising. The arrowhead grew heavy and he put it back into the tin on the floor beside him, to look at in the daylight. His eyelids were beginning to grow heavy again and his thoughts were becoming muddled. He opened his eyes for a moment, trying to remember where he was. Why was he in this warm, stuffy, cluttered room? Then he gave up trying to think at all, and slept.

3

The Dream

For an hour Rob slept heavily, tired out by exhaustion. The bed was lumpy. He was hot under the blankets and half woke to push them down a little. He had been dreaming, and was not quite sure whether he was awake or whether the stuffy, dimly-lit room was part of the dream.

Then, still half-asleep, he remembered that he hadn't been indoors at all in the dream, but out on the mountainside with the sun on his face and grass under his feet. It hadn't been February, either, but autumn, for the leaves on a clump of hawthorn trees were turning yellow and the berries were crimson and ripe. The air held the sharp clean tang of an early frost.

He thought he was sitting on something near the hawthorns—a tree stump or a fallen trunk, and could clearly see a cluster of creamy-yellow fungus clinging to the wood near his feet. Strangely, his feet were bare and rather muddy, but didn't seem to be cold. Beside him was a tool of some kind, something heavy and cool and hard that he had been working with, but had laid down for a moment. The cooing of wood-pigeons sounded from the trees, and there was a smell of wood-smoke in the air.

The dream was so vivid that Rob wanted badly to stay in it, to go on with the thoughts he had been thinking as he sat under the hawthorns with the yellowing leaves and ripe red berries. He felt he had been on the verge of some new and exciting discovery and struggled to retain the thread of his thoughts, or dreams, or ideas. But already it was fading, the bright sunshine giving way to flickering firelight, the cool sharp open air to the confines of an overheated small room smelling of sheep.

He was sweating. He pushed the blankets further down so that his arms were outside them. He wondered what the time was, but the grandfather clock stuck persistently to ten past four and the old man's pocket watch was across the room on the dresser. He decided that he would go across and look at it. Old Amos had moved to the other armchair by the fire with its back to the doorway and was asleep, head back and snoring a little. But his sleep was light and he woke immediately Rob swung his legs over the edge of the bed and stood up.

'Be you all right, boy?'

'Yes. Sorry to wake you up. I was going to look at the time. Do you think it's almost morning?'

The old man got stiffly to his feet. 'Nowhere near yet. About twelve or quarter past, I'd say.'

In his T-shirt and boxer shorts, Rob walked across and picked up the watch. 'Quarter past twelve, spot on!' he said. 'How could you tell?'

'You gets to know the feel of the time of night, stopping up lambing,' said the old man sagely. He yawned and stretched his arms. 'You feeling better now?'

Rob was disappointed that it was still only just past midnight, with a long night still to go before he could go home. But he found that he'd stopped feeling sick and that his headache was now quite gone. He was feeling better all round.

'Yes, thanks,' he said.

Amos got to his feet and went to inspect the sick ewe, who got up, looked at them both with a kind of weary patience, and lay down again in a different position.

'It wouldn't surprise me none if her lambed before morning,' prophesied the old man.

On his way back to bed, Rob remembered the dream he'd had. For some reason he felt he'd like to tell Amos about it. He said, 'Before I woke up, I was dreaming I was out on the hillside, sitting carving or sharpening something.' Suddenly he remembered quite clearly what it was—a piece of stone or flint which he had been shaping and honing to a sharp point with some other tool. He said, 'It was an arrowhead—like the one you showed me.'

The old man's bushy eyebrows lifted with interest. 'Ah. That took your fancy did it, that old arrowhead. I thought them things in the tin would interest you. What did you think to the old medals then? Did you dream about them too?'

Rob shook his head. 'No. I wasn't dreaming about any of the things, exactly. It was more—more as if I was really there, back in time.'

Amos nodded, settling himself back into his chair. 'Ah. That's easy to do, that is. Specially as you gets older. You'll find it easy to go back in time when you gets to my age.'

Rob swung his legs into the bed and lay down, pulling up the covers. He wondered again how old Amos was, and decided he would be considered rude if he asked. Instead, he asked, 'Have you lived here a long time?'

'All my life, I have, man and boy. Eighty-seven I be, come next May.'

He chuckled creakily and went on, 'Eighty-seven years I've lived here. All my life in this self-same house. And my father before me. And his I daresay. I don't see no purpose in moving around like folks does today.'

Rob lay silent. He thought that if his own age was added to the old man's, it would be a hundred. A hundred years. A century. He could hardly imagine such a span of time.

The thought of countless generations, stretching back and back, all keeping sheep on this mountain, made Rob feel rather confused. Or maybe it was because he was growing sleepy again. For a while he thought again of the dream... Was the boy in the dream himself, or was it some other boy who had lived long ago, much longer than even Amos could remember, when the arrowhead was new and sharp? He wished he knew.

Amos was nodding off again. For a moment, as sleep came, Rob thought he heard a voice call his name, or some other name, but probably by then he was already dreaming.

4

Cuckoo Time

Circa 3400 BC

Overhead, the sky was the clearest of blue, the blue of the eggs of a song-thrush, with not a cloud in sight. Squinting a little at the sun's brightness, Rac lay on his back on the sweet new grass beyond the clump of hazels. Far up beyond the hazel catkins and the froth of white bloom on the wild apple trees, the tiny dot of a solitary skylark hung against the blue, sending its bubbling song back to earth. Other birds were twittering and building in the hawthorns and hazels, and as Rac listened, he heard from somewhere far away in the oak forest the unmistakable call of a cuckoo, the very first that year.

He let out his breath in a long sigh. Cuckoo time—the Warm Time, here to stay at last, after many false starts ending in wild storms or bitter sharp frosts. Time to leave their snug winter caves and move to the open country, to the clear air of the mountainside, its woods and forests teeming with game ripe for the hunting. Wolves would stay far from their new settlement, nights would be mild and days long from Fire-Rise to Fire-Down.

He sighed again, a sigh of deep content, and dozed a little in the warmth.

'Rac! Rac!'

He jumped awake. It was his stepmother's voice, out of temper, with the sharp note that would have heralded a beating if he had been just a little younger and smaller. Even now that he was taller than she, his father's wife was not above giving him a sharp clout with her hand or whatever else was within reach. Guiltily he raised himself on an elbow and peered cautiously through the hazel stems and sprouting undergrowth.

Dru, his stepmother, and the other women were erecting the summer shelters near the spring. They were light, flimsy constructions of branches and boughs with mud plastered in the clinks. The men had already left on a hunting trip. Several children were running about supposedly fetching and carrying mud from the spring and small branches and twigs, but more often getting in the way. The other older boys had gone with the men, but Dru knew her stepson. Even at this distance she looked cross, hands on hips, as she scanned the hillside for some sign of him.

Rac flattened himself in the undergrowth, tempted to ignore the call. Dru would have some work for him to do, and he wasn't that keen on women's work. The trouble was, he wasn't that keen on what the men did either, neither the hunting nor the fighting, though he was a Headman's son and almost old enough to be a warrior himself. He would much prefer to be on his own, making his pictures, watching the small secret lives of the birds and insects and small creatures, and maybe knowing again the special warmth and joy of the Presence that sometimes came when he was alone.

'Rac! Rac!'

The voice sounded tired as well as angry and his conscience suddenly smote him. It was hard, toiling in the warm sun, and everyone ought to do their share. He bounded to his feet and sprang down the hillside with long loping strides to the new settlement. Dru looked cross and weary, her dark hair escaping in damp tendrils from its bone ornaments. She seemed to lack even enough energy to box his ears or berate him for being a 'dreamer'. Rac expected to be given a job on the half-built Chief's hut, but instead she said, 'The day's half over and there's no meat. The men won't be back until Fire-Down. Go and look in the traps. There should be a kid, at least.'

She turned back to the hut. Rac's heart gave a little leap of joy. Walking the trap-line was much more welcome on a fine day than roofing huts with ash branches. He flashed a beaming smile at his stepmother's drooping back and bounded off across the springy turf on strong legs before she could change her mind.

It was an uphill climb to the dark sprawling mass of the oak forest, slantwise across the lower mountain slopes, up to the nearest ridge and down the other side. Above him the familiar bulk of the mountain rose steeply, dark purplish blue meeting the clear blue of the sky along the sharp line of its ridge. A thick carpet of heather and whinberry bushes, which later would yield tiny sharp-tasting berries, clothed much of the mountainside, in between patches of short turf, bright yellow gorse bushes and grey outcrops of flinty stone. From somewhere deep in the forest the cuckoo called again.

Rac was sweating profusely by the time he reached the trees. His heart beat faster as he plunged into the cool green depths, alive with springing new leaf and bud, and sweet with birdsong. Little paths branched off here and there among the thickly tangled undergrowth, made by wild pig and wolf, deer and human feet. There was danger here, he knew, and not just from wild beasts. Other tribes than his were on the move, settling in new summer homes, establishing the new season's hunting and trapping runs, and only too ready to do battle with a neighbour.

Rac sighed, padding along silently on a layer of last year's leaf-mould. What was it about the ending of the Cold Time that seemed to stir men's blood and make them want to begin again to fight and steal and kill? He didn't know. What he did know was that any member of another tribe whom he met in the forest would just as soon stick a spear through him as not, without troubling to ask questions first.

There was nothing in the first pitfall, built by himself and his father the day before and carefully concealed by boughs and bracken. He covered it again and moved on to the next, deeper in the wood. He saw at once that something had fallen in here, raggedly breaking the camouflage. But he let out a grunt of surprise as he bent to peer in. Instead of the expected kid or small pig, a strange animal lay crumpled and dead at the bottom. He blinked and peered again. He had never seen a creature like it. It was thickset and short-legged, with a close-curling brownish coat and horns that curled back and inwards towards its shoulders. Its neck had been broken by the fall, and in the heat a mass of buzzing flies clustered blackly around its mouth and nose.

Rac sat back on his heels, one thought following another.

The thing was strange, but fat, and probably edible.

It had a good thick coat, for clothing and footwear.

It was heavier than a deer, too large for him to pull out alone.

He would have to get help.

He was getting to his feet when a new sound came to his ears. A high, plaintive sound, like the crying of a baby. He stopped to listen, and it came again. His eyes darted around the undergrowth for signs of movement. Suddenly his scalp prickled with the feeling that he was not alone, that from some hiding place other eyes were watching. Then a trembling in a clump of ferns caught his eye, and from it emerged another of the strange creatures, a miniature of the dead one, but without horns and with longer spindlier legs, giving out the high bleating baby cries. It did not run at the sight of him but stood hesitantly and then came towards him. He guessed that it was the young one's mother who lay dead in the pitfall.

It was no trouble to catch the youngster by its

soft neck and it hardly struggled. He did not kill it at once, but decided to take it home alive to show to the others. Its smell was strange, slightly greasy, and its coat had a greasy feel too. It ought to make a tasty stew for tonight, which would please his stepmother. A couple of men would come and pick up the dead one. Perhaps they would know what kind of animal it was.

The small creature flopped limply in his arms, its legs dangling. As he tucked it under one arm, the feeling that he was being watched came again. He made his way towards the edge of the wood half expecting at any moment to feel a spear in his ribs or an arrow in his back, or at least a bellow of rage. But there was nothing, just the twittering of forest birds and the sound of his own breathing as he lugged home the orphaned young animal.

5

Secret Valley

The small creature was heavier than it looked. It seemed a long way home, and Fire-Down had almost come by the time Rac reached the new settlement.

Immediately he walked in with his burden, he was surrounded by an inquisitive crowd, first the children but soon joined by the older members too. He dumped the animal on the ground and rubbed his aching arms.

'What is it?'

'Is it a new kind of deer?'

'Where did you find it?'

'It's a strange thing. Will it bite?'

Hands reached out to poke and prod and squeeze. The young creature struggled to its feet, bleating and bewildered. Rac picked it up and held it, suddenly protective.

'Get away! Leave it alone!' He aimed a kick at a small boy who was yanking the woolly tail.

Rac's stepmother Dru looked pleased. 'It will make two days' stew. And a good pair of leggings for a child. Maybe shoes, too.'

When Rac started for home it had been with much those intentions in his own mind. Now he felt a sudden strong distaste for the idea of slitting the animal's throat and stretching its soft brown hide to dry on a curing frame. He held it a little tighter and said, 'I had thought to keep the small one until it grows. We have the dead large one for meat and for the skin.'

Two men had already set off to retrieve the dead mother. Dru and the others stared at him. Then Dru said, with a covetous look at the animal, 'It would eat much and take long to grow large. And it might run away. Or be taken by a wolf some dark night. Then we would have no benefit of it at all.'

Stubbornness rose in Rac. 'I would care for it. Keep it from wolves. It's not like a fawn. See, it doesn't run from me.' He added cunningly, 'When it is grown, it will make many stews. And many shoes and leggings.'

Rac's father spoke from the doorway of the new shelter. 'The boy speaks good sense. Let him keep the small one until it grows large.'

Rac looked at his father with surprise and gratitude. It was always hard to predict Neb's moods. His father's face wore its usual surly look, but Rac felt a rush of warmth. Someone had once told him that Neb had felt it very hard when Rac's mother died, and had changed from a cheerful man to a morose and bitter one. Rac had no memory of the cheerfulness. But he thought that he would offer to clean and polish Neb's spear and axe for him after supper.

During the long journey home, clutched in Rac's

hot sticky arms with its soft nose absorbing the smell of him, the young creature had decided that Rac was now its mother. When he put it down it followed him on wobbly legs. The other children screamed with laughter at the sight. Some of them longed to poke it with a stick or throw stones at it, but he threatened them with his fists, and they kept their distance. He found a bit of soft deerskin for a collar and fastened it about the creature's neck. It watched him trustingly and nibbled at his hands and knees, until he realized that it was hungry. He did not know how to feed it, and after a while it lay down in a corner and went to sleep.

The larger creature was brought in, examined, skinned and dressed to the accompaniment of much curiosity and speculation. No one had seen one of its species before or knew what it might be. They took the heart and liver and some of the ribs and roasted them on hot stones for supper. The meat was good and tasty, and left a faint film of grease on mouth and hands. Wiping his fingers afterwards, the fullness of his stomach reminded Rac that the young one must be fed, too, if it was to live.

The examination of the teeth and the stomach contents of the larger creature had told that the strange animals were eaters of grass and vegetation. Rac pulled handfuls of new grass, sweet and tender, and held them to the young one's mouth. But it only turned its head away, bleating its pathetic baby-cry and trying to nibble the boy's fingers. Its small stomach rumbled with hunger.

'It is too young,' said Dru, watching. 'It would feed from its mother. It cannot chew its food yet.'

Inspiration seized Rac. 'Then I can chew for it.'

He crammed a handful of grass into his mouth and chewed, after a while spitting the wet green mess out into his hands. The small animal was no more interested than before, but reluctantly swallowed when Rac forced open its mouth and pushed the mixture down its throat. He was bone weary, and the Fire-in-the-Sky had sunk to the edge of the world by the time he judged that the creature's small stomach was full enough.

Now Rac spent his days with the young creature at his heels. It followed him wherever he went, like a dog. But whereas the hunting dogs were mostly snappish and cringing, Rac's creature was merry and carefree. It soon began to frisk and toss its head, kicking up its heels and butting him playfully with the small hard head where little knobs that would later be horns were beginning to form. It thrived on its diet of pre-chewed grass and soon began to nibble for itself on grass and dandelions and tender shoots and buds. It could be quite a nuisance, nosing into the shelters where it had no business, butting and climbing and nibbling and causing annoyance. Rac sometimes tethered it by a long throng to a hawthorn tree, but it bleated so pathetically that he could not keep it tied for long.

The days were lengthening and Neb and the others were planning a raid on another tribe which had settled somewhere along the edge of the oak forest on the hillside above them. The smoke from their cooking fires could be seen, though none of Neb's tribe had seen the people.

'Why?' Rac asked his father one day, when there had been much eager talk of a battle. 'Why must we attack them?'

His father looked surprised. 'Don't be stupid. That is the way. If not, they will attack us. Who strikes first has the advantage. You should know that.'

'But what for? What good is it? People killed, people hurt, shouting and blood. All for a few pots and pans or a piece of deerskin or two. Or a woman for someone needing a wife. We have pots and skins enough. We have women here. There is meat enough for all in the woods. There is space enough.' He waved his hands at the blue bowl of the sky above them, the vast expanse of the hillside and the towering mountain range beyond, and sat down suddenly on a hillock, rather surprised at the length of the speech he had made.

His father scowled, fashioning the tip of an arrow from a sharp flint. 'You talk too much. That's the way things are. There's no other way.'

'Why not? There could be. If we made another way.'

Neb's dark face flushed, embarrassed by this kind of talk. 'Quiet, now. You shame me with this talk. I am too soft with you, I think. Maybe I should beat you oftener.'

Rac sighed and got up, chirruping to his animal to come to him. It was no use talking. The men would go on just as they always had, keeping their weapons sharp and encouraging each other with tales of past victories. Showing old injuries, like the puckered scar down Tira's cheek and the mutilated hand of One-Thumb, who had lost all the fingers of his left hand in a chop from a stone axe. The boys not yet warriors would listen, building up their own fighting spirits, waiting for their own time. Nothing changed.

Meanwhile, his growing creature was in trouble again.

'It has overturned my stewing-pot and broken a bowl!' screamed Dru, bursting in a rage from the shelter. 'It is nothing but trouble! I should like to see its throat cut and its quarters curing in the smoke!'

She brandished her skinning knife. Neb turned away, unwilling to become involved in domestic crises. He was also a little afraid of the sharp edge of Dru's tongue.

Rac decided it was time to make himself scarce. He grabbed the frayed end of the tether and dragged his creature away, out of the settlement and off up the hillside to his own secret place.

This was almost half a day's walk away, over ridges and through hollows, to where a rocky outcrop jutted out against the sky. Climbing here alone one day in the last Warm Time, Rac had discovered a small tunnel, just big enough for a crouching boy, leading into the hillside. Crawling a distance into it, he had seen light ahead, and found it led not to the expected cave but to a lovely little valley open to the sky. High rocky crags surrounded its edge, but on its floor grew the softest and springiest of grass, starred with wild orchids and lady's smock, with a cluster of gorse bushes and even a pair of hawthorns, frothy and fragrant with bloom. A family of young rabbits had stared curiously at him before scuttling away, and a thrush had its nest in one of the hawthorns. No other of his tribe knew this place. It was his very own.

In the secret valley smooth stone walls rose steeply all round, perfect for drawing on. He had always loved making pictures, in the dust or mud or on walls or scratched on stone. No one else had any patience with his scratchings, and some laughed at him. So he had begun to come alone to his secret place to draw and paint. The rock walls held many of his pictures—in yellow or red ochre, or white chalk, or scratched and chiselled with a flint tool. Pictures of birds and animals and trees and flowers, of men hunting or fighting, women working and cooking, children playing, all he knew.

It was here, all alone last Warm Time, that he had first been aware of the Presence—some unexplainable sense that he was not really alone at all, but that Something—Someone—larger and more powerful than he could begin to imagine, was there too, something that was also warm and caring and meant him only good. The first time he sensed it he had looked around, sure that someone else had found the secret way into the valley. But he was alone, except for the warmth and peace that came with the Presence. When it faded, he had yearned after it with a sense of desolation. He had run home with the tears wet on his cheeks.

But the Presence had come again and again, almost every time he looked for it. When he drew his pictures he had the fanciful thought that in doing the very best he could he was pleasing the Presence. But he did not speak of it to anyone.

Now he crawled again up the tunnel, dragging the creature behind him on its lead. They emerged, and the animal at once kicked up its heels and frisked the length of the valley, before settling to graze. The hawthorn was in bloom again, creamy-white and buzzing with wild honey-bees. Rac's pictures glowed from the walls. He had brought a sharp flint tucked into his belt and planned to begin at once on a new picture, of a small creature with a long tail and a woolly coat. But even as he reached for the flint, he felt himself grow tense. He knew suddenly that he and the creature were not alone in this place. His eyes darted round the craggy tops, the bushes—and suddenly there was a movement among the gorse. Next moment the prickly branches parted and a small figure rose from among them.

6

Lamb?

It was a girl who emerged from the gorse, a strange girl, smaller than himself, with a cloud of dark hair and large brown eyes fringed with long lashes. She wore a red-dyed skirt and a necklace of boar's teeth and in her ears were ornaments of carved bone. She stared calmly at him, and for a moment Rac was too amazed to move or even speak.

After a moment his hand tightened instinctively on the handle of the sharp knife at his belt. He heard his own voice say, 'You are not of our tribe. I will have to stick you through with my knife.'

He saw that the girl carried no weapon, but she seemed unperturbed by his threat. She said quite calmly, in a small but sweet voice, 'No, you will not.'

Her speech was not quite like his own, but like enough for Rac to be able to understand. His mouth gaped a little and he felt very much at a loss. He said at last, 'Why do you say I won't? You don't belong to my tribe, and this is my place.'

He glared at her and gripped the knife, but the girl

only smiled, a quick sweet smile that lightened her rather wistful expression.

'It isn't only your place. I come here too. But you won't stick your knife in me. I have seen you. Many times I have seen you.'

Rac could only gape wider in astonishment at this girl, who seemed not in the least afraid of him, though he was a superior male from another tribe, and armed. He stuttered, 'I—I have never seen you. When have you seen me?'

The girl laughed, twirling a strand of her long dark hair.

'Many times! I have seen you climbing the hillside and cutting wood and setting your traps. I saw when you took the small one away with you. I have seen you come to this place, and I have seen you make your scratchings on the walls.'

Rac gulped. This amount of information was too much for him to digest all at once. He said lamely, 'You see a lot!'

The girl laughed again. He gathered together his wits and said with a show of fierceness, 'I still think I should stick you through.'

'Why?'

Rac was reminded of his earlier conversation with his father. Like Neb, he was at a loss to reply. He said, still stuttering a little, 'Because—because you are of another tribe, and I don't know you, and—and you are only a female—'

Even to his own ears his reasoning sounded foolish. He said feebly, 'Well, maybe I will let you live. For a little while, anyway. But you must tell me everything I ask. What are you called?'

'I am called Bara,' said the girl in her sweet voice. She fondled the ears of Rac's pet, which was butting playfully at her knees with its long tail wiggling.

'That creature belongs to me,' said Rac loudly. He added, 'But you may touch it if you wish. I am called Rac. I am the son of Neb, the headman of our tribe.'

'I know,' said Bara, scratching the small woolly head. 'I am the child of a chief too. And this lamb is not your creature. It is ours.'

Once more Rac was lost for words. His mouth gaped again. She had given the creature a name. Lamb. And said it was not his.

His hand went again to his knife. 'That is not the truth. I have raised this small one myself. Since its mother died in our pitfall.'

Bara sighed, her eyes rolling upward with exaggerated patience. 'Yes, yes. All this I know. I watched you that day by the pitfall. But that dead sheep was ours. The lamb is really ours.'

'Sheep? Lamb? These are strange names,' said Rac warily. 'I have never heard them. How can this be true?'

'Truth does not depend on *you* knowing it,' said the girl pertly.

This was too much for Rac. He glared, his hand on the knife, knowing that somehow this girl was making a fool of him, but not quite knowing how. She seemed to take pity on him all of a sudden, and said quickly, 'I will let you keep the lamb, even though you have eaten our ewe and cured its skin. No one else knows. It was our fault anyway that they strayed. We have others. I have three all of my own, like that small one of yours.' Her hand went to a small skin bag on a thong round her waist. 'Are you hungry?'

Rac realized that he was very hungry indeed, having gone off in a hurry and given no thought to his noon meal. He said, again in a loud voice, 'Yes. If you have food, you must give it to me.'

He reached for the skin bag, but Bara stepped back and held it just out of his reach. She opened it and divided the dried deer meat and small flat barley loaves between them, offering some crumbs to the lamb, who licked them up. They ate the food sitting together on the warm grass under the hawthorns, while the bees buzzed in the creamy-white blossom and the Fire-in-the-Sky rose to its peak.

'I will go now,' said Bara, when they had eaten everything. 'If you are not going to kill me. Perhaps you will want to scratch some more marks on the rocks.'

'Yes,' said Rac. He felt full and contented, but the thought suddenly came that the valley and the afternoon would lose something of its brightness if the girl went away. He said, 'I shall make a new picture now. On that bit of smooth rock over there. But you need not go away. You may stay and watch me, if you wish.'

Bara smiled, and he thought that really she was rather pretty. She scattered the last crumbs of food for the birds, and then stood quietly at his shoulder, watching as he worked on the surface of the rock with his flint knife, chipping and chiselling out the likeness of a young lamb on the hard greyness. She turned her head this way and that, admiring the likeness as it took shape, and caressing the head of the real lamb every time it came close. The afternoon wore on, and the Fire-in-the-Sky dipped down to one side of the blueness above the valley.

At last he stood back to look at the finished work.

'It is very like,' said Bara admiringly, reaching forward to trace the lines of the hooves with her fingers. 'Almost I think it could run and jump like this small one here. You have great cleverness in your hands and in your thoughts.'

Rac looked at her, quite overwhelmed. No one had ever admired his work before, or called him anything much other than idle and shiftless and a dreamer. He struggled to find some way of showing his gratitude.

'Maybe next time I will make a picture of a girl in a red skirt, with a necklace of teeth and hair reaching past her elbows.'

'Oh!' Bara clasped her hands in delight and her eyes sparkled. Rac was glad he had not stuck his knife into her.

It was time to go. Rac rubbed his flint knife on the grass and stuck it back into his belt, and called the lamb to attach its tether. Bara collected her food bag and some wild orchids she had gathered. They crawled down the tunnel and emerged onto the hillside where the late afternoon shadows were lengthening. A thought came to Rac suddenly. 'Where is your settlement?' he asked.

Bara pointed towards the oak forest, where a faint plume of smoke showed beyond the trees. 'There. On the edge of the wood. There is good grass there for our sheep.'

Rac was silent. The knowledge sprang into his mind that Bara's village was the very one Neb and Nolo, the tribe's Wise Man, and others were planning to attack. He opened his mouth to speak, but hard on the heels of that thought came another: if I tell her, she will go home and warn the others of her village. Then they will hide their women and children and goods, and we won't get many spoils. They will prepare their weapons and strengthen their defences. They may even attack us first, some Fire-Rise when we are still sleeping and not expecting them. He closed his mouth again and pressed his lips tightly together.

'I must go,' said Bara. 'I have work to do, and my lambs to feed and make safe for the night. Maybe you will come here again—'

She did not wait for a reply, but turned with a flash of her red skirt and ran, her feet nimble among the whinberries and heather. Rac watched her go until her small figure was swallowed up in the gathering dusk.

7

The Raid

'New Fire-Rise but one is the time,' said Neb to his son.

Rac felt a sickness in the pit of his stomach. 'Time for what?' he asked, although he was only asking to gain time. The two of them were skinning a buck, killed by one of Neb's spears shortly before. Rac's father glowered at him across the half-flayed carcass.

'You know what, boy! Why ask?'

Rac had seen his father and Nolo, the tribe's Wise Man, in close conversation that same morning. He knew that Nolo had decided upon a propitious day for surprise attack. The face of Bara sprang into his mind, with its long-lashed dark eyes and sweet smile. He said, 'Fighting is a waste of time. Better to save our good weapons for the hunt. And our strength for work. How can men work and hunt with wounded legs and chopped fingers?'

His father stared at him. 'A new thing indeed, for you to worry about work! Are you afraid, boy? Of the spears and arrows of others?'

Rac felt his skin flush. It was not pleasant to be

thought of as a coward. He said, 'I see no need of killing. If we want more skins or pots, why not offer something in exchange? If women for wives, why not ask?'

Neb straightened up and laughed loudly, hands on hips. He tapped his forehead with a forefinger. 'Your mind is addled, boy, by too many scratchings! Ask for them, indeed!' He doubled over with mirth at the thought.

Rac swallowed an angry retort. 'Maybe,' he said carefully, 'the people in that village just want to be left alone. To live their own lives. Care for their sheep.'

'Sheep? What is sheep?'

Rac gestured at his lamb, lying in the shade of a hazel chewing the cud. 'Like that one. Only large, like the one we ate. Many can be herded together. The ewes have milk, good to drink. And if a male is there—a ram—then young ones every Warm Time. More skins, more milk, more meat for the Cold Time.'

Neb's mouth was open in astonishment. 'I think you are dreaming again. Creatures run wild and have to be hunted. And if we were to keep them, it would be women's work. Not fitting for warriors.'

Rac gave up. There was no arguing against his father's set ideas. He thought of telling him about Bara and the people of her village and their sheep. But that might only increase the desire to kill and steal.

But later that afternoon in the secret valley he told Bara about the planned raid. They had met there often since the first time in the long light days of the Warm

Time. Bara listened in silence, twisting the necklace of boar's teeth. 'So,' she said in a small voice, 'that is how it is. Did you not try to persuade your father not to do this? I thought you agreed with me that killing is senseless.'

Rac's fists clutched in frustration. 'I did try. But he wouldn't listen.'

'Then what?'

Rac thought for a moment. 'Then we must attack, I suppose. What else?'

'And your people will kill mine?'

'Not all of them,' said Rac quickly. 'You can warn your father, and you can hide yourself. And hide your sheep. Besides,' he brightened at a sudden thought, 'if you were captured, you would be our slave. In our house. Dru is always saying she has too much work.' The more he thought about this idea, the more it appealed to him. He wanted to say, 'And in a handful more Warm Times you could be my wife.' But the thought made him hang his head with shyness. Instead he said, 'Dru is not too bad. She would feed you well and would not beat you more than once a day.'

'Indeed!' said Bara with a flash of dark eyes. 'That I do not care to find out!'

They were silent for a moment.

'What will you do?' asked Rac at last.

Bara sighed. 'I will warn my father, of course. They will be ready for your attack. It will be a mighty battle. They shall not easily take our sheep.'

Rac felt sick again. 'Can you not hide them?'

'A flock of sheep cannot be easily hidden.' She

sighed again. 'The night before, they will feast and dance, and implore the spirits. Do your tribe make sacrifice before battle?'

'Yes,' said Rac. 'A young hind, mostly.' He was reminded of an uneasy thought that had been bothering him since the morning. 'Although I did not like the looks that Nolo was giving my lamb today.'

He felt Bara give a little shiver. She was silent for such a long time that he thought she had fallen asleep. Then she said, 'Almost, I think I should take my own three sheep and go away, many days' journey.'

'But you could not. Not alone. There would be danger.'

Bara tossed her head with a flash of spirit. 'I could try. Better to be killed by wolves than to be stuck through with one of your spears. Or to be a slave.'

'But where?'

Bara rested her chin on her hand, deep in thought. 'Once, last Warm Time, some of us were lost in a thick fog, the sort that comes down suddenly. We wandered far away until we could scarcely walk for weariness. When the fog lifted, we saw that we had come to a pass leading between the two highest mountain peaks.' She pointed to where the huge bulk of the mountains towered against the blue sky.

Rac held his breath. 'And was there land beyond? Or just nothing?'

'There was land. A beautiful valley, green and fertile. A river running through. More hills beyond.' She looked at him. 'Much sweet grass for sheep to graze.'

'But...' Something was struggling in the back of Rac's mind, an idea that would not surface. He said, stuttering a little, 'But—you would be alone. That is not good. Not safe. And I—would be left.'

Bara's eyes were bright. 'You could come with me.'

Rac's mouth gaped. This was the idea that had been struggling to be born. Bara was watching him carefully. She said, 'You could bring your one lamb and I my three. Yours is a ram and mine are all ewe-lambs. In another year we could begin our own flock. There is good grazing in that valley. We are both strong and can hunt. And build ourselves shelter. You could paint your pictures and scratch your marks.'

Rac closed his mouth and digested this series of ideas. Suddenly he realized that this was what he wanted more than anything. He said, 'I will come! Wait while I go and get my lamb!'

He sprang to his feet as though he would start immediately. Bara put out a hand to hold him back. 'Wait. Not yet. We must get together some goods—food, and extra clothing, weapons and tools. I will manage to warn my father of the attack. Then, at Fire-Down tomorrow, when all are preparing for the battle, we will slip away.'

8

Blizzard

Rob woke with a start and shot upright in the bed, pushing back the covers. It was quite dark, except for the faintest glimmer of red from the fire's dying embers.

He was confused, but knew that he had slept too long.

'It's dark! Fire-Down has come! We must start!'

In a panic he half-climbed, half-tumbled from the bed, catching one foot in the blankets and banging his head against the wooden bedpost. In all the commotion, the dog leaped to its feet and moved quickly to the side of its sleeping master. Old Amos woke with a startled grunt. The ewe in the pen let out a frightened bleat.

'Here, here. What's all this, then?'

The old shepherd struck a match in shaky fingers and held it to the wick of a candle standing in a pewter candlestick on a chest by his side. The small bright flame made a pool of light around the hearth and sent flickering shadows moving in the dim corners of the room.

Amos looked at the boy standing confused and blinking beside the bed. 'What's all the shouting about? The fire's gone down a bit, but it bain't out, quite. I'll soon stir it into life. What's the matter with you, boy? You cold, or summat?'

He rose and poked at the fire, riddling the dead grey ash down through the grate and throwing on a dry split oak log. The red embers glowed and small flames from them licked up at the wood with a crackling sound. Rob noticed that his wet jeans and sweater and jacket had been spread to dry on a string stretched from side to side across the mantlepiece.

Rob wasn't cold at all, just bewildered and somehow feeling cheated. He had been dreaming again, he knew, and in the dream there had been sheep, and arrowheads, and some kind of threatening danger, and a girl—a girl with long dark hair and laughing eyes.

It was the girl he remembered most, and it was she who was in danger.

He stumbled towards the door, still half dazed with sleep.

'I've got to go. We must start.'

'Go? You bain't going nowhere, for a bit. Take a look outside and see what it's like.'

Amos took Rob's arm and pulled him over to the window, drawing back the curtain. Rob peered out, blinking. A fierce wind was hurling snow against the window. It spattered with savage force against the glass before sliding down to join the ever-growing heap of snow piled up on the window-sill. Rob saw that the snow had changed from large, soft, feathering flakes to small, hard, solid, icy particles. Beyond the window he could see the snow driving relentlessly in the dim square of light, choking the sky, piling in drifts against walls and buildings, cutting off farm from farm and neighbour from neighbour, isolating each in a freezing, whitened world.

He blinked again, reality returning in a series of jolting thoughts that were almost painful.

He was at Ty Mynydd, with a blizzard blowing outside in the darkness.

He wasn't Rac, but Clive Roberts—Rob to his friends—of Penvaen Farm down the valley.

He'd been having a dream.

Amos let the curtain fall back again across the window.

'It's a fair licker!* I ought to go out and look at the lambing ewes in the building, by rights. Three o'clock, that's about the time I usually goes. But I reckon I'll leave it a half-hour or so, to see will it ease up a bit.'

Rob didn't answer. He was struggling with a strange feeling of disappointment, almost loss. Amos put on another log and put the kettle on to boil.

'You want more cocoa?'

'No, thanks.'

Rob sat down on the chair opposite Amos and looked at the flames dancing blue and yellow as they took hold of the dry logs.

'No need to look so miserable, boy. We be safe enough and snug enough here for the night.'

'I suppose so.'

---
* 'It beats everything!'

The old man cocked an eyebrow at him. 'It bain't anything to fret about, you know, being snowed up. Like I told you, they'll have a helicopter out, soon as it clears a bit.'

Rob hadn't been fretting about that at all—in fact, the possibility of being snowed up hadn't entered his head. They'd been snowed up often enough at Penvaen and it was no big deal, though maybe it was a more serious matter up here, more than a thousand feet above sea level.

Rob no longer felt homesick, but he realized suddenly that his family had no way at all of knowing that he was safe and well. It might be several days before he was traced, and by then he knew that Mum would be frantic. For the first time he considered how desperately anxious and frightened his family would be.

Again, old Amos seemed almost to read his mind. 'You believe in him upstairs, boy?'

'Upstairs?' For a moment Rob was nonplussed, wondering if Amos had someone else concealed in the bedrooms of his little farmhouse. Then he realized that the old man meant God. He was startled for a moment, remembering the last thought he'd had before losing consciousness out in the snow. He said, 'Do you?'

The old man nodded several times, slowly and thoughtfully. 'Aye. Went to the little chapel across the mountain for nigh on sixty year, I did. It closed down in the end, only two or three were going. Weren't worth the preacher coming out from town. But I still worships here, in my own way.'

Rob thought of the small church in town that he and his family went to faithfully every Sunday. At least, his parents were faithful. Just recently he'd started finding excuses to wriggle out of going whenever possible—a sore throat, a pulled muscle, even an extra load of homework.

The thing was, he was beginning to wonder whether all that going to church and praying was a waste of time. He wasn't at all certain that God was real. Or if he was, he had the feeling that God had no time for him, Clive Roberts, because he certainly didn't answer his prayers any more.

Amos' knack of following on from Rob's thoughts seemed quite uncanny. He said, 'I says my prayers regular, chapel or not. Very often times like now, up in the night with a ewe.'

'And does God answer you?' Rob hadn't intended to ask that, but the words were out almost before he realized.

'Oh aye, he do answer. Not always in the way I'd ha' thought. But always there's an answer, in time.'

They were both silent, while the fire crackled and the wind whistled and moaned and threw bursts of snowflakes against the windows.

Rob knew that the old man was trying to tell him that prayer was the thing to do in a situation like this, where there was nothing else to be done. Suddenly he had an overwhelming urge to tell old Amos everything, about that stupid row with Nick and the awful thing he'd done and the guilt and fear that had followed. How he'd prayed and prayed, until at last it seemed there was going to be an answer, but then the hope had been cruelly snatched away again.

Rob cleared his throat. 'Amos, have you got a family?'

The bushy eyebrows cocked again. 'A family. Oh, aye. My missus ha' been gone near on fifteen years, but I ha' got a daughter. Her's in Australia, but her writes regular. Wants me to go over there to them, but I couldn't go from here. Megan's married to a sheep-farmer over there, and they says I could help out with the shepherding if I went. But t'wouldn't be the same. I couldn't stick the heat. Never liked hot weather, myself. Nor the moskeeters and all the insects. And I'm too old to change my ways now.'

He put a gnarled hand down to touch the sheep-dog's head, and she thumped her tail and licked upward at his fingers. The dog was a black-and-tan border collie bitch, old and wall-eyed, and Rob guessed that she was specially privileged.

'Too old to change, aren't we, Floss?' said the old man. He went on, rather wistfully, 'It'll be near on ten years now since I seen Megan. My grandsons was bits of nippers then, when they last come over. Wouldn't know 'em now, I daresay. One of 'em's on the farm with his Dad—they calls it a station there—and the other's in the Air Force.'

Rob sat up straight in the armchair, leaning forward eagerly. 'My brother's in the Air Force—the RAF. The second oldest one, Nick. The other's an HGV driver.' Suddenly the words were tumbling out, tripping over his tongue in his eagerness to talk. 'Nick's an engineering technician, working on the big transport planes. He works on the airframes and on the engines too. He's a corporal now and might be a sergeant before long—'

He paused for breath, his heart thumping with relief at being able to pour all this out at last. He went on, 'Nick's really clever, he was top of his group at training school. He won all sorts of prizes. He does all kinds of sports as well and he's not scared of anything—'

He gulped, because a big lump had come up in his throat.

The old man had been listening intently. He said, 'I reckon you're real proud of your brother. Miss him, do you?'

Rob swallowed the lump and nodded. 'I haven't seen him for a long time—' And then suddenly he couldn't say any more, because his eyes were full of tears. He bent his head so that the old man wouldn't see.

Rob had already made up his mind that he was going to tell Amos the whole story, even if he broke down and cried like a girl and made a real fool of himself. Something in him seemed ready to melt, like the candlewax that was softening and melting and running down the sides of the candle in the pewter candlestick.

But just then several things happened at once. The sheep in the pen in the corner seemed to waken all of a sudden, coming to life with a strangled bleat and a threshing of limbs. Floss pricked her ears and raised her head from her paws, and Amos got up more quickly than Rob would ever have thought possible. He bent over the ewe and examined her in the flickering candlelight.

Then he said, 'Quick, boy! Reach the oil-lamp down for me and then put the kettle on to boil. Her's going to lamb, and I might need a bit of help.'

9

Twins

Rob had watched the births of many lambs and assisted at several, but just the same he marvelled at the skill and gentleness with which the old man, speaking soothingly and gently to the ewe, helped her through the long and difficult birth.

It was twins. One of them, the first-born, was in a difficult position. Rob found himself kneeling in the straw beside the ewe, steadying her head and holding her still when she began to thresh about in pain and bewilderment. Amos manipulated and pushed and turned the difficult lamb, until at last it emerged slimy and steaming into the straw. The other was easily delivered and followed almost immediately, at once vigorously shaking its head and struggling to get up on to its long dark spindly legs.

The first lamb lay limp and apparently lifeless in the straw, and at first Rob was quite sure it was dead. But Amos knew better. Grunting and puffing, he took an old hessian sack and began to rub the lamb vigorously with it. The ewe was already bleating weakly and turning her head to look for her new offspring. Rob took the sturdy second lamb and placed it near her head, where she began at once to nuzzle it and lick it clean.

'Will that one live?' he asked.

'Oh, aye. He'll come all right, give him time. Needs to get his circulation goin', that's all.'

Nevertheless it took a lot of rubbing, stimulating the lamb's body and moving its limbs until they were rewarded at last first by a sneeze and then by a feeble baby-bleat. The mother answered at once, turning from her newly-washed second-born to look for the other one. The old man picked it up, head and legs dangling limply, and put it at her head where her tongue could reach it. Rob saw that the old man's hands were shaking and that his face was grey with fatigue and dripping with perspiration. He felt hot and shaky himself, despite the fact that he wore only his underwear and that a blizzard blew outside. Lambing was always hard work.

He said, 'Shall I put the kettle on again, Amos?'

The old man had given the ewe a drink and a dose of black medicine from one of the bottles on the mantelpiece. He got up stiffly from his knees, breathing hard, and went to wash at the sink in the corner. 'Aye, you do that. Make us a cup of tea for a change. And then I ought to go and look at the other ewes by rights. It's near on four o'clock.'

Rob made the tea and brought a mug to Amos, who had lowered himself wearily into his armchair and was leaning back exhausted with his eyes closed. His hands shook as he took the mug from Rob, dripping a little tea on to the rag rug in front of the fire. 'Times like this I do feel my age. Maybe I ought to have a drop of brandy in it before I goes out in the cold.'

Rob noticed that Amos' face still had a greyish tinge in the glare from the hissing paraffin lamp. He said, 'I don't think you ought to go out in the cold at all. I'll go and see the ewes for you. I know what to look out for.'

Already he was pulling on his jeans, now almost dry from the heat of the fire. Floss, who had been bored and disinterested through the lambing process, jumped to her feet and stood expectantly near the door.

But old Amos would have none of it. 'No, boy, you stop here! I've pulled you in half-starved once tonight and I don't reckon to do it again. You go back to bed or sit quiet by the fire and don't go from there. It's not fit for man nor beast, out of doors this weather.'

'Well then, it's not fit for you to go out either,' said Rob. 'And you haven't been to bed at all.'

'I'll go just now.' The old man's jaw took on a stubborn set. 'You get on and rest now. Don't go fretting about me.'

Rob felt an answering stubbornness rise in himself. The two of them sat facing each other in the armchairs. Rob thought that when the old man dozed off he might nip out with Floss and take a look at the ewes. At the very least, he would insist on accompanying the old man if he ventured out to the sheep shed. Maybe there was no real need at all, and the ewes would be perfectly all right until daylight came, when perhaps the storm would have died. In the corner, the two new-born lambs had already struggled to their feet and suckled, and had now folded their long spindly legs under them to rest at their mother's side.

Rob felt a sense of relief when the old man's head drooped forward and a gentle snore sounded from his lips. For a while he'd been quite worried about the grey and exhausted look on Amos' face, the sweating and the pinched look about the old man's mouth. He got up and tiptoed across to the bed, took a blanket and tucked it gently around Amos. He hesitated for a moment, wondering whether to go back to bed, but decided against it. He'd sit up in the other chair, and when it began to get light he'd go and take a look at the sheep for Amos.

He wrapped another blanket around himself and made himself comfortable with his feet on a low footstool. The fire was dying again, but he thought he'd be warm enough for a while. He'd make it up again when daylight came, before he went out to the sheep shed.

His thoughts were getting muddled again, coming in confused waves between periods of blankness.

He'd left the lamp on. He should have put it out really, to save fuel.

He hoped that Mum and Dad and Pete would soon know that he was safe and well.

He'd get up and put out the lamp when he'd rested for a few minutes.

By the time sleep came, his thoughts had somehow turned again to a boy and a girl preparing for a long journey.

10

Time to Leave

Fire-Down came at last at the end of a long hectic day of intense preparation. Almost from dawn the men had sat with their weapons, polishing and honing spears, sharpening arrowheads, tightening bowstrings. All the time tales of previous battles, in which they had always proved victorious, flew thick and fast.

Dru and the other women had been busy too, mixing coloured dyes for the painting of faces in preparation for the ceremonies to follow, and preparing a great feast. Large stones had been heated in the fire, to be dropped into the stone cooking troughs for boiling water in which cuts of deer and wild pig would be stewed with herbs. Other joints would roast over the red-hot embers. Some of the women were busy mixing and kneading the cakes of barley-meal and honey, to be baked on large flat stones beside the hearth. The children had been busy for days, gathering mushrooms and hazelnuts, ramsons, Jack-by-the-hedge, crab-apples, blackberries, rosehips, and other varieties of ripened autumn fruits to add flavour to the feast. An air of excitement grew over the settlement. Several moons had waxed and waned while they waited for this day.

Rac watched with mixed feelings. Whenever he could he went off to make his own secret preparations. Often he was called upon to transfer a heavy cooking-stone, or to bring more water from the spring, or to fetch and carry in half-a-dozen different ways, but in between he had collected a skin bag full of food which no one would miss at a time of such abundance. He had managed to hide it safely under a pile of stones along the route he and Bara would take when it was dark, together with a spare tunic and leggings and his sleeping cover of deerskin. He made a strong new thong to fix to the collar of his lamb, now well-grown and long-coated, but still playful and devoted to Rac.

Early in the afternoon Neb came across his son sitting under the hawthorns sharpening his spear. Neb's dark face broke into a rare expression of pleasure. He said, 'I am glad to see you preparing for battle, son. It is now your time to be a warrior. I did not really think you were a coward.'

Rac's heart moved. He bent his head over the spear haft to cover his confusion, and kicked at the creamy yellow fungus growing round the base of the dead log on which he sat. He did not know what to say, yet he badly wanted to say something, because the thought came that this might be the last time he and his father would speak together.

He found himself asking something about which he had long wondered. 'Father, your first woman, the one who was my mother—I have sometimes thought I would like to know about her. How she looked, and how she was.'

For a moment he thought his father would be angry. No one ever spoke to Neb about his first woman, and only seldom, and very quietly, among themselves. But Neb's hard face softened.

'She was like you. Not in looks—she had lips as red as those hawthorn berries and hair like a crow's wing, and you are an ugly cur—though you might improve with age. But she was apt to dream over the cooking pots. Sometimes I thought that she heard and saw things that others could not hear and see. She liked to sew patterns in beads on the deerskin clothes. She made little pictures on birch-bark—'

He stopped suddenly, unused to speaking in this way about the woman whom he had clearly loved much. He looked sideways at his son, half ashamed at this disclosure of weakness.

Rac held his breath. He fully expected his father to turn surly again and fetch him a clout. But Neb only looked sad, and rather weary, as he gathered up the quiver of flint-tipped arrows he carried. Then he seemed to pull himself together and gave Rac's shoulder a brisk slap.

'That is a good spear point you have made. After tonight you will be a man. I may be proud of my son, after all.'

He turned away. Again Rac felt his heart twist. He raised his head. 'Father—'

'What now?'

'Father—I am already proud to be called your son.'

But he knew that really he was saying goodbye to his father. Neb nodded his thanks as he strode away. Rac felt a hot tear trickle down his cheek and splash onto the ash haft.

Throughout the whole day, Nolo, the tribe's Wise Man, had stayed alone in his hut, a little apart from the others in the settlement, muttering and brooding. Rac was more afraid of Nolo than he was of anyone. He had never seen Nolo's face and nor had anyone else as far as he knew. All anyone saw was his glittering eyes that showed through the slits in his deerskin mask. Tonight Nolo would emerge, wearing his stag's antlers as well as the mask, with the rattle-stick in his hand, and this would be the sign for the festivities to commence. Nolo held powers far greater than those of Neb, the Headman. He even had power to punish with death those who broke the tribal laws.

Rac shivered a little, thinking of Nolo. He knew what would happen if he was discovered trying to run away from the village. No one was ever allowed to run away, especially if he happened to be a Headman's son. Rac knew that if he was caught his body would end up high in the branches of one of the tall oaks, left there until the flesh left his bones, with his feet pointing towards the rising Fire-in-the-Sky.

He tried to make his mind think of other things, going on with his preparations. As the day wore on the warriors painted their faces in lurid stripes of blue and yellow, red and white. The fires burned bright, and the great cooking pots sent out tempting odours of roasting and stewing meat and fresh-baked barley bread. Towards Fire-Down two or three of the young men took skin drums and began to beat a soft tattoo.

As darkness fell, Nolo emerged at last from his hut, a terrifying figure in his antlered headdress over straggling grey hair, a rabbit-skin cloak around his shoulders and a necklace of bears' teeth around his neck. He held his rattle-stick in one hand and a long bone club in the other. For a moment he stood surveying the scene with glittering eyes, and then raised the rattle-stick high with a fearful noise. It was time for the pre-battle festivities to begin.

It was not too difficult to slip away under cover of the drumming and the dancing, the shouting and eating and drinking and boasting. Children were running everywhere, in and out of the legs of their elders, dangerously near to the fires, stealing whatever bits of food they fancied. Even the dogs got their share, cringing in the shadows near the edge of the firelit circle and sneaking closer whenever they dared. The drumming grew louder and more hypnotic, the dancing more frenzied.

Nolo and a group of the warriors were studying omens, examining the shapes of crows' entrails thrown in the dust to see what they foretold for tomorrow's battle. It was time to leave, and Rac did so, melting away into the darkness at the edge of the firelight and hurrying to untie his lamb from its tether and lead it unnoticed away through the gathering dusk.

11

The Great Spirit

Rac found Bara waiting at the place, with her three half-grown lambs and her bundle of possessions. Beyond a brief greeting they did not speak, but hurried away from the village, avoiding Bara's own village at the edge of the dark mass of the forest and heading for the looming mountain range. The sounds of drums and voices throbbing in unison followed them, getting gradually fainter as they began to climb. Above them the sky had darkened to a deep midnight blue and the stars were beginning to come out. Rac's lamb followed nimbly and willingly on its lead, unperturbed by this strange turn of events. Bara's sheep did not even need to be led, but kept close at her heels, pressing against her legs on either side whenever she paused.

They stopped at last to draw breath, having climbed steadily for a long time. It was quite dark now, with only a thin sliver of new moon to give a little light. Below, in the valley, a small bright patch of orange flame showed where Rac's village lay. The occasional burst of sound came faintly through the still air, men's voices chanting in rhythm, the throbbing of drums, broken now and then by a shout or a shriek. Further across the hillside, half-obscured by the forest, another patch of fire flickered and danced. Rac knew that this was Bara's village. He felt her give a little shudder beside him.

Their hearts were thumping fast, both from the climb and from the experience of being out alone on the hillside in the darkness. Neither had ever been away from their village, from the fireside, after dark before. Thoughts of strange spirits of the night came unbidden into Rac's mind. Evil spirits could be more easily kept at bay in the light of day; in the darkness who could tell what dreadful things might creep up and come close? Who knew what the spirits might choose to do? He put his arm round the woolly neck of his sheep and held it close for comfort.

For a moment, the summer shelters of home, with their leafy roofs and warm smells of cooking and babies and animals, seemed to beckon him to return. He wondered if he had been missed yet. There was no way of telling, but, if so, there would be no return.

'We cannot go back now,' he said.

Even thought it was quite dark he knew that Bara had turned her head to look at him. 'Do you want to go back?'

'No. But—'

'If you do, you can go. There's still time. No one would guess that you've been running away.'

'No, no. Unless—'

'Unless what?'

'Unless you want to go back. It was your idea to go, but I have noticed that sometimes women change their minds.'

He felt her toss her head. 'I don't change mine! But I can go on without you if you wish.'

Somehow they had come to the verge of a quarrel, although Rac had no idea how it happened. He searched very hard for something to say that would make things right again.

'I was just sad for a moment, thinking of my father. Are you not sad to leave yours?'

She was silent for so long that Rac feared she had fallen into a sullen mood and was refusing to speak to him, though this had never happened before. He said humbly, 'I'm sorry, Bara. Sometimes I speak like a fool.'

She touched his hand. Both their hands felt chilly in the cold air. 'No, no. I am not angry. Just thinking about my father, too. Yes, I am sad to leave him. He has been a kind man, mostly. But—in the end, I could not stay.'

'Could not?'

Bara said, in a choked voice as though she might weep at any moment, 'Yes. Could not. You see, in our village, as in yours, it is the custom to make sacrifice before battle. But whereas you sacrifice a young creature, we—we offer whatever is most precious. It could be the best hunting dog or the fattest and best young ram. But—I heard our Wise Man speak to my father, when I should not have been listening. He told my father that he has seen that his only daughter means much to him. My father said nothing, but, I think—I think—'

'That he would have sacrificed *you*?' asked Rac in horror.

Bara gulped. 'Perhaps. He is an honourable man. He wants his people to have victory in battle. But—I did not want to die, not yet.'

It was Rac's turn to shiver. He reached for her hand again. 'It was a good thing we thought of going away!'

Bara gave a little sound, half sob, half laugh. She gave his hand a squeeze. 'Yes, it was a good thing.'

They got up and climbed again, first pushing through tall fronds of bracken just turning brown, later wading through dense low-growing whinberry bushes and heather. It was hard going, with just a thin gleam of moonlight to guide them. The sheep grew tired of the uphill walk and hung back, panting. Towards dawn they found an outcrop of rock jutting from the mountainside and huddled beneath it, boy and girl and sheep together.

Tired as they were, sleep did not come easily at first. Rac felt strangely vulnerable and unprotected in this cold, dark, lonely place. He felt he, as the male, and elder, should be protective and strong and fearless, but instead found himself saying, 'Do you think the spirits will be angered, too, as well as our people? That we have fled?'

Bara's head was resting against her favourite ewe-lamb, the youngest and smallest, who kept as close to her as it could at all times. She said, 'I don't know. We have done nothing to cause anger. Only wanted life, and peace. Why should the spirits always want war and bloodshed? And, indeed, why should we have to do what the spirits want?'

Rac glanced around uneasily at the darkness, wondering if they were being overheard. 'That is dangerous talk. Do we not need the goodwill and help of the spirits in what we are doing?'

Bara was silent for a moment, hugging her knees. 'I'm not sure they have goodwill. Or that they help us. Except, the Other—'

She paused. Rac strained his eyes to see her face in the moonlight, but it was obscured by a cloud of dark hair. 'The Other?'

'Sometimes,' said Bara, drawing a deep breath, 'sometimes, when I smell the petals of a primrose, or listen to the bleating of a new baby lamb, or look at the black clouds gathering when a storm is coming—'

Rac held his breath. 'Yes?'

'Then, I feel—that there is a Great Spirit—greater far than any of those they sacrifice to—and that, although he is larger than the mountain, larger than the sky—that he knows me by my name and cares for me. That he is not angry and vengeful like those others, but kind, and so strong—'

Her voice tailed away uncertainly, as though she was half afraid that Rac would laugh at her. His heart began to beat faster. 'This—Other. This—Great Spirit. Does he come—did you feel him—in our secret valley?'

She turned towards him, speaking fast and eagerly. 'Oh, yes! Often there! But not only there. Out on the hills, too. When I am tending the sheep, or lying down to sleep. Why? Have you felt him too?'

Rac nodded slowly. 'Yes. In my valley often, when I did my drawings. It must be the same. I thought it was only there, and only me. But if, as you say, anywhere—' He caught his breath. 'Then, here, with us, now?'

She nodded, her eyes shining with excitement in the moonlight. 'Here. Now. Everywhere. And kind, and strong, and knowing us. We can speak to him, and he hears.'

'He will help?'

'Yes.'

A great peace seemed to settle over them both. Wrapped in their deerskin covers and warmed by the bodies of the lambs, they slept as peacefully as though they had each been at home on their beds in the huts of the village headmen.

12

The Cave

Rac and Bara woke to find themselves looking down on a swirling blanket of white fog which completely blotted out the lower slopes, including the oak forest and their own two villages. Fire-Rise was long past and the Fire-in-the-Sky had climbed high up and had already dried the night's mist on the mountainside. Its traces lingered in fine droplets of moisture on their hair and clothes and eyelashes, and on the woolly coats of the sheep, but already the air was warming.

Rac stretched himself and reached for the bag of food. The sheep had scrambled up and were cropping at the short sweet mountain grass. A wind-stunted rowan dangled its bright scarlet berries encouragingly, and somehow everything seemed brighter and more hopeful in the light of a new day.

Bara sat up smiling. 'You see. Now, even if our people wanted to come after us and bring us back, they could not, because they are smothered in that thick fog while we have the Fire's light and warmth and can see our way clearly. Didn't I tell you that the

Great Spirit would care for us?'

Rac decided that it was too early in the morning for any deep discussion of spiritual matters, but he felt his own spirits rise. Just for a moment he thought of the mighty battle which must have taken place at Fire-Rise. Had the dawn raid been successful? He wondered if his father was still living, or if he had been wounded or maimed, and how many others were suffering chopped fingers or spear wounds or other painful injuries. How many families had fathers or brothers missing on this new day? And what of Bara's family? It was probable that they would never know.

They rationed out the morning's food carefully, for they still had a long journey ahead. They let the lambs eat their fill before leading them forward again. All drank from the clear water of a dewpond.

Travelling was very much easier in the daylight and they made good progress, always climbing the long, whinberry-covered slopes towards the pass in the far distance glimpsed between two of the high mountain ridges. As they climbed, the air cooled, and by afternoon there was a nip in the air that they had not noticed before. Towards Fire-Down Rac stopped and sniffed the air like a hunting dog.

'What is it?' asked Bara.

'It smells like snow,' said Rac.

'Snow? There won't be snow yet. It's much too early in the year. The berries are still on the trees, and most of the leaves. It's been a warm day.'

'Not up here,' said Rac. 'We've climbed all day, and

we're still climbing. We must have reached the snow-line. The peaks are often white at this time, remember? There could be snow before we reach the pass.'

Bara shivered. 'I hope you're wrong. I don't like snow. I hope it won't come.'

Rac hoped so too. Travelling the mountains was difficult enough without that complication. But the wind was getting keener the higher they climbed, and he knew that whether it snowed or not they were going to need more than a little rocky outcrop for shelter that night. He began to search for somewhere before Fire-Down and darkness came.

Not long afterwards, he had his first suspicion that they were being watched, or even followed. Stooping to drink from another of the little dew-ponds glittering in the grass, he jerked suddenly upright again at a rustle from a thick clump of gorse bushes nearby. A rabbit shot out suddenly from the bushes and ran in panic in front of them and disappeared into a hole in the hillside. Rac's keen eyes scanned the darkening scene.

'Bara,' he said, 'we have flints for making fire, don't we?'

She looked up at him from where she had flopped to rest. 'Yes. Why? Do you think we should have caught that rabbit and cooked it to save our food?'

But Rac was not thinking of fire in connection with cooking, though it was a good idea. After all, the trip might take longer than they'd thought, especially if there was snow, and their food would not last for ever. But Rac's fears were much more immediate. He was almost sure he'd seen something grey and alive, moving among the undergrowth a good way downwind of them, keeping concealed from view but nevertheless following their tracks and keeping pace with them. He said nothing to Bara. There was no need to frighten her, maybe without good cause. But he kept his eyes moving in all directions for the sight of a suitable cave. There were many natural caves in the mountainside, especially as the ground became higher and more rocky. But the one he wanted had to be dry, and out of the wind, and deep. Deep enough to hold two people and four sheep, with a flat place at its mouth to build a fire for the night.

They found a suitable cave at last, burrowing deep beneath a huge slab of rock. It was not quite high enough to stand in but it was deep and wide with a dry sandy floor. Rac saw with relief that there was even a supply of firewood to hand, where a mountain ash had uprooted in a spring gale and lain drying all through the summer. And a pond lay clear and sparkling not far away.

'We must chop this wood first of all, and stack it inside for our fire,' said Rac.

Bara was tired, and would have liked to rest and eat and drink before beginning work. But Rac was insistent. With the tools they had brought they hacked the ash boughs into manageable lengths and dragged them into the cave.

'Do we need so much for just one night?' asked Bara.

'Yes,' said Rac. Both were warm from the exertion,

but the wind was keen and biting. Again, sniffing the air, he smelt that chilly taste of snow he had noticed earlier.

'You start the fire, there in the cave mouth,' he said. 'I'll carry water and store as much in our pots as we can.'

Again Bara gave him a questioning look, but got out the flints and gathered dry twigs and branches without comment. Soon a small but cheerful fire was crackling in the cave entrance.

The four sheep were grazing again, pulling at the short grass near the dewpond. Bara's ewe-lambs made a tight little group in which Rac's lamb was not yet included. He stayed a little distance away from them, knowing that they would run at him and butt him with their hard little heads if he got too near. It was a game they played, without much malice, but the lamb was not quite convinced of that yet.

As Rac stooped to fill his leather bucket at the pond, he was aware that the wind had suddenly changed its direction, blowing directly from the north. As it changed, so did the attitudes of the sheep. All at once they forgot their differences and banded together, leaving their grazing and pressing into a tight group, breathing fast in panic through dilated nostrils. From its changed direction the wind had brought a new scent to them, something that filled them with terror.

At the same time the wind, driving full into Rac's face, brought with it the first cold stinging handful of snowflakes.

13

Wolves

Bara was crouching inside the cave, setting out some of the food from their packs. She took one look at Rac's face and asked, 'What's wrong?'

Rac didn't answer for a moment. He had carried the buckets of water in each hand, at the same time herding the four sheep ahead of him back to the cave. They had scuttled along quite willingly, their ears flicking fearfully backwards and forwards as they listened for some new sound. They paused for a moment at the sight of the crackling fire, but they were used to fire and didn't object when Rac drove them past and into the cave, where they huddled in a group at the far end, their eyes gleaming in the firelight. Rac hung the water buckets carefully on a rocky projection inside the cave mouth.

'It's snowing,' he said.

Bara looked at him. Already they knew each other very well, well enough to know when the other one wasn't telling everything. She said, 'Yes. I know. What else is wrong?'

Rac looked at her large eyes with the firelight's reflection in their depths. 'I think—I'm not sure, but I think—we may have been followed for some time. By wolves.'

Bara nodded. 'That is why you wanted a cave, and fire?'

'Yes. Of course, they may not come here after us. It was the sheep they were smelling, the sheep they would like to kill. And maybe there is only one of them,' he said hopefully. 'But they begin to run in packs at this time of the year, when the Cold Time is coming.'

Bara nodded again. 'Well, we're safe here, us and the lambs. We can even cook food, now we have a fire.'

The prospect of a hot meal put new heart into both of them. Bara had brought with her a cooking pot, small but big enough to cook a meal for two, and they found smooth stones to heat and drop into the water. Soon some strips of dried deer meat were simmering gently, together with a wild onion and a pinch of the dried herbs Bara had brought. The savoury smell made their mouths water. They rested while it cooked, making themselves comfortable on the soft sandy floor with their bundles of clothes and covers to cushion them against the hard rocky walls. Outside, the wind was rising to a gale, but the cave was snug and well-sheltered, and soon cosy and warm from the heat of the fire. The sheep forgot their earlier panic and lay down to rest and chew the cud.

Outside, in the circle of light cast by the fire, Rac and Bara could see the swirl of snowflakes, tiny moving dots that danced and whirled and flung themselves recklessly into the flames. When Rac got up to take a closer look, he saw that the snow was already sticking, piling at the side of the cave entrance in the beginnings of a drift. The storm showed no signs of slackening. He began to be worried again. This kind of blizzard, even an early one, sometimes went on for two days or more.

'It will still be fine, down in our villages,' he said.

Bara seemed to have quite forgotten her earlier distaste of snow. 'Pooh! What is a little snowstorm? We are warm and dry here. And we have our thick boots to walk in when the snow stops.'

Rac was worried about the lack of grass to feed the sheep, but he didn't voice it. In any case, he felt much better when the stew was cooked and they had fished out the meat with their fingers and chewed it hungrily, and then tilted the bowls to drink the good hot broth.

They put more wood on the fire, feeling pleasantly full and relaxed. Rac was almost tempted to think that it would be quite safe for them both to lie down and sleep, warm and snug, until the morning. But he said, 'I will watch for a time while you sleep. Then, if you wish, you can watch for a while.'

Bara nodded and yawned. She was asleep in seconds, curled in the deerskin cover on the dry sandy floor with her head on the woolly flank of her favourite pet lamb. Rac propped himself against the wall just inside the cave entrance and watched the flickering flames and whirling snowflakes.

His head drooped and he dozed a little. He dreamed of a large hut full of strange objects, fire, a whirling snowstorm outside and sheep of a strange breed asleep nearby. He was propped up half asleep himself, but woke in a panic knowing that something was missing. He was quite alone except for the sheep. Bara was not there.

Rac's head jerked up and his eyes flew open. His heart was thumping with terror. Where was Bara? Then he saw her, sleeping peacefully on the floor of the cave with her cheek cupped in her hand. He had been dreaming, that was all.

He reached for more wood to put on the fire, which was dying low. And then he saw the eyes, yellow in the firelight, glittering not six feet away from him just outside the fire at the cave's entrance. He was on his feet in an instant, shouting and waving the ash branch he held. The eyes retreated, but only a few feet, staring unblinkingly at him. Straining his own eyes through the whirling flakes, Rac thought he made out several dim crouching forms.

He heaped wood upon the fire, trembling. The shapes retreated a little further.

Bara was at his elbow, shivering a little. 'Is it wolves?'

'Yes. They've tracked us here.'

'The fire will keep them away. Won't it?'

'Yes.'

But Rac was already measuring with his eye the stack of firewood, judging whether it would last the night. In the morning the wolves would retreat and go away to lie up for the day, he hoped. They were night creatures as a rule, and not often known to attack humans.

It was the sheep they were after.

Bara said, 'It is the sheep they smell. Or maybe it was the smell of our stew cooking that drew them here.' She shuddered and looked back over her shoulder into the dark cave. The sheep were all on their feet, terrified, pressing as tightly as they could against the furthest wall.

Rac said, 'They are safe here. We must just make sure that the fire is kept bright, and we shall all be safe.'

'Yes.'

They were silent for a moment, watching the flames leap and crackle, fed by the dry ash. Then Bara said, 'I have already had a good sleep, so I will watch now and feed the fire while you take your turn.'

But Rac could not bear the thought of Bara watching alone with the yellow eyes of the wolves gazing hungrily from beyond the fire. In the end, they decided that both would watch together. They settled side by side near the cave mouth, wrapped in their covers.

As the night wore on the wolves crept back again, sitting in a half-circle around the cave entrance and the fire. When the fire burned low they ventured even closer, creeping low on their bellies like the sheepdogs of Bara's village, drawn by the smell of food inside the cave. The snowflakes settled on their thick coats and now and then one of them would rise and shake itself free of snow. When a fresh branch was placed upon the fire, blazing and crackling with a shower of sparks, they retreated a little. But they didn't go away.

'There is nothing to say that they will go when daylight comes,' said Bara in a small voice.

It was the dark hours before dawn. Their hopes had sunk to a low ebb and their fears had risen to the surface. The same thought had been in Rac's mind for some time. But he looked at Bara's anxious face and said stoutly, 'They will go, sooner or later. We just have to wait.'

But his words sounded hollow, even to himself. If the wolves stayed, they would be trapped inside the cave. The pile of firewood was getting smaller, and when it was gone there would be nothing to stop the wolves entering the cave.

Despite the danger of their desperate situation, Rac found it increasingly hard to keep his heavy eyelids open. He wondered whether after all it might have been wiser to take turn and turn about in their watching.

His head drooped a little to one side and he was dozing. But suddenly a new sound jerked him fully awake, his heart thumping with fresh terror. A dreadful crescendo of sound filled the dark night air. Beyond the firelight, in the falling snow, the circle of wolves were pointing their noses to the sky and howling in chorus.

14

No sign of life

A cinder fell with a rattle from the dying embers in the grate, and Rob woke with a start. He had been dreaming of wolves—wolves pointing their noses to the sky in a snowstorm and howling in unison their desolation and frustration. He rubbed his eyes. The snowstorm was real enough. The sound of it whined around the old farmhouse with wearisome persistence and icy particles of snow slithered and scraped at the window. He straightened suddenly in the big chair, because the howling was real too. All the sheepdogs in the outbuildings were raising their voices together in a sobbing, wailing crescendo.

Rob flung aside the blanket in sudden panic. He was alone in the room, except for the sheep and her lambs in the pen in the corner. Floss was gone from the hearthrug. And old Amos was gone from the opposite armchair, out into the storm.

Rob grabbed his sweater from the drying line and began to thrust his arms into the sleeves in desperate haste. He was mad at himself for falling asleep again when he'd tried so hard to stay awake, and hopping mad at the old man for sneaking off by himself like that, when he'd refused point-blank to let Rob go.

The ewe got to her feet in alarm as Rob blundered about the dimly-lit room finding his jacket and socks and boots. She shuffled her hooves and stamped defiantly at him in defence of her young, looking much stronger and fitter herself since giving birth. Remembering the grey, pinched look on the old man's face, Rob hoped desperately that he wasn't struggling alone out there in the cold outbuilding with another difficult lambing.

When he opened the porch door the storm hit him with such force that he tottered for a moment before he could pull the door closed behind him. Stinging snow burnt his cheeks and driving wind snatched his breath as he stood trying to get his bearings. It was pitch black and the blizzard showed no signs of abating. Snow was piled in deep drifts along the walls of the house.

A large mass looming even darker through the whirling blackness must be the outbuildings where the in-lamb ewes were housed. The wailing and sobbing of the dogs' chorus seemed to be somewhere in the same direction. The sound might serve as a guide. Rob had picked a small pocket torch off the dresser, but its light seemed thin and puny against the driving darkness. After a step or two he found himself floundering, up to his knees in deep snow. He staggered up and pressed ahead, keeping his eyes on the bulk of the building. No light showed, not even a chink round the edge of a door. Where was Amos?

It seemed to take a long time to cover just a few yards, battling all the way against the force of the wind. His cheeks and hands were icy-cold almost at once and his eyes watered. Then suddenly he came upon Floss, almost falling over her where she sat directly in his path. Half covered with falling snow she sat there in the beam from his torch, her nose pointing skyward and howling in a way that made his flesh creep. It was probably her noise that had set off all the other dogs.

Rob began to feel a horrid apprehension. Floss never stirred from her master's side, kept her eyes on him always.

Where was he?

Flicking the torch's beam from side to side, he saw a mound at the edge of a deep drift just ahead. An awful suspicion clutched at him with icy fingers. He bent and began to scrabble at the snow covering the mound.

The first thing that showed was a glimmer of light from Amos' powerful torch. It must have fallen from his hand and been completely buried in the snow. As Rob removed handfuls of snow, the beam of the big torch, still shining, showed suddenly like some ghostly phosphorescence among the whiteness. Rob pulled out the torch quickly and set it to one side with his own, their combined beams pointing towards the drift to give light. He could see now that the long mound was the size and shape of a man.

Frantically scrabbling at the snow, he uncovered

first the back of a head clad in an old woollen balaclava, and then the collar of the old Army greatcoat that had hung behind the living-room door in the farmhouse. He worked quickly to clear the snow from the face, a sick trembling in all his limbs. Was the old man alive or dead? Could a person breathe when they'd been lying face down in the snow like this, for goodness knows how long? He must have been there for quite a long time for the snow to have completely covered him.

Floss had stopped her mournful howling and was whining eagerly, waving her tail and pressing forward to lick her master's face. As if a switch had suddenly been pressed, the other dogs stopped their noise too. The only sound was the moan of the wind and the terrified thumping of Rob's heart.

He could see in the torchlight that Amos' eyes were closed. His face felt stiff and icy-cold to the touch. Rob was almost certain now that the old man was dead. He felt a sob rise in his throat, and his eyes were full of hot tears. He said aloud, in a choked voice, 'I should have stopped him. I should have.'

Then he thought he heard a new sound, a soft moan in response to Floss's licking tongue. He threw himself down upon his knees beside the buried man and scrabbled frantically at the snow again, shaking the overcoated shoulder as he uncovered it, tugging at the arm, which dropped limply when he let to go again.

There was no flicker of life on that weathered old face, just flakes of snow settling to be licked away by Floss's warm tongue.

Suddenly Rob was angry, angry with the blizzard, angry with the relentless falling whiteness, angry with the heavy cold blanket that covered and buried the body of the old man. He began to scoop and dig at it with his bare hands, pushing away mounds of it, scraping and scrabbling it away from Amos' lifeless form. He felt the tears overflow and trickle down his cheeks, making warm runnels through the coldness. Away somewhere over the mountain tops to the east the very first rays of a chilly dawn were beginning to filter through the whirling blackness, but Rob did not notice. He was convinced that the old man was dead, but was somehow determined that he should not be buried here under the drifts, with no one to know and no one to care. With all his might he fought the blizzard as though it was some ferocious devouring animal.

And then he heard two things.

Another faint moan, and a joyful burst of barking from the old sheepdog.

15

Hope

Just one moan, and the faintest flicker of an eyelid, but it meant that Amos was alive! There was still hope.

Rob redoubled his efforts, scooping and clearing the snow from above and around the old man's body. Amos must have slumped forward into the drift when he fell, so that the piled snow had cushioned and protected him from further injury. More snow had fallen to cover him, and this had probably acted as insulation against the cold and the biting wind. Maybe his feeble breath had melted the area around his face, just enough space for air to keep him alive.

Rob could see now that a grey and wintry dawn was beginning to break at last. The blizzard seemed to be slacking off a little too. The air was not quite so choked and full of whirling snow and the wind was dying a little. He felt a surge of hope. If he could get the old man into the warmth and safety of the farmhouse there might be a chance that he would survive.

The problem of how to get Amos back to the farmhouse struck Rob just as he succeeded in digging him out of the drift. The old man hadn't moved at all. He was lying face down in his Army greatcoat, an old sack over his shoulders and gumboots on his feet, his face, as much as Rob could see of it, an awful shade of greyish-white with an ominous blueness about the lips. Rob tried to drag him from various angles, by the shoulders, the arms, even the legs, while Floss danced around, cocking her head in puzzlement at this performance.

But it was hopeless. The old man was a dead weight. A boy of Rob's size and strength couldn't manage to move him more than an inch or two by pulling, and couldn't lift him at all.

Rob gave up and sat in the snow, sweat trickling on his body under his clothes, close to tears of frustration. He had only succeeded in moving Amos' limbs a little, and now he lay spreadeagled, like some grotesque obsolete scarecrow tossed down in the snow. Rob could hear the old man's breathing now, an ominous snoring sound that somehow frightened him more than the silence. He knew that Amos might die at any time, and probably would whatever he did.

Yet he couldn't give up, not just like that. There must be some way. There came into his mind fragments of the conversation between himself and Amos, earlier in the night. They'd talked about God, and about prayer. Strangely enough, Rob had thought about God when he'd been lost in the snow himself. Had God led him to Amos' remote farmhouse? Or was everything down to chance?

He wondered if he should pray for Amos, for help in

saving his life. But he couldn't see what good it would do. No one would come here at this early hour, before it was properly light. Even a mountain rescue helicopter, searching for Rob himself, would wait until proper daylight before venturing out in these treacherous conditions. Rob had no doubts that they'd find him eventually, and he knew there was plenty of food to survive on in the farmhouse until help came. They'd find him all right. But by then it might well be too late for Amos.

His mind returned again to prayer. He'd have to try it, there was nothing else left to do. He'd better begin properly, explaining before he made his requests that he wasn't quite sure about God any more, or, at any rate, that God still cared—

Rob began to form the words in his mind, but before he could speak them he looked again at Amos. The old man's face seemed suddenly to have shrunken, fallen in upon itself. The snoring breathing was growing fainter and shallower. The wrinkled cheek lying against the snow pillow looked blue-white and transparent.

He was dying.

A sob burst from Rob's lips. 'God! Oh, please! Please don't let him die! Help him! Help me, oh, help, help!'

In his desperation his voice had risen to a hoarse shout. Floss pricked her ears, and in the building across the snowbound yard the young sheepdogs burst into a fresh frenzy of barking.

A picture came into Rob's mind, clear and sharp

and detailed, breaking through the turmoil and fear. A moderate snowfall, not as heavy as this but giving a good covering, several years ago, the last real snow they'd had until now. Trees, boughs laden down with the weight of it, each branch and twig covered with a fairytale coating of white. Himself, younger and smaller, and a younger Nick, climbing the steep field above the farm, warmly wrapped in woollen hats and mittens, their breaths cloudy in the cold air, cheeks rosy from the cold. Climbing and climbing, panting with exertion, pausing now and then to throw handfuls of snow at each other. Some had gone down Rob's collar and he'd thought fleetingly about Mum's wrath, but it didn't matter, nothing mattered but the glittering brightness of the day and the joy of his brother's company. They'd sledged down the hill, again and again, sometimes colliding on the way down and nearly always ending up falling off in a tangle of arms and legs and helpless laughter at the bottom of the slope.

But they had not been using a real sledge, because they had left it out half-concealed by snow a day or two before and Dad had accidentally run over it with the tractor and hadn't had time to mend it yet.

They had been using empty red plastic bags, the type used for livestock mineral supplements, the very same kind that Amos had in a pile in one corner of his cluttered porch.

Rob scrambled to his feet and began to plough his way back towards the house. Floss hesitated, unsure of whether to follow or to stay beside her master. Then she looked at Amos and sat down firmly in the snow beside him.

It was getting light now, a cold wintry grey dawn revealing a glistening white landscape. Now that the snow was stopping, the extent of the fall could be seen, stretching away in unbroken whiteness over the mountainside, piled and heaped into deep drifts along two sides of Amos' farmhouse, reaching almost to the window panes. Away from the buildings, the wind had whipped snow into strange shapes, pinnacles and swirls and cones like giant ice-cream cornets. A still cold silence followed the noise of the storm.

In the porch, Rob seized the nearest red bag and hurried with it, floundering through the snow, to where Amos lay. He placed it one the snow beside the old man, scooping out a long hollow at a slightly lower level first.

Even the task of turning the old man over seemed at first beyond Rob's strength. He heaved and tugged, getting a grip on the Army greatcoat and then losing it again as Amos' weight dragged him back. Panting, Rob at last got the shepherd on to his side, his back to the red plastic bag. One more push, and he toppled over onto his back on the plastic, falling limply like a rag doll, not even his eyelids flickering.

Rob got a grip on the end of the bag near the old man's head and pulled. It was hard, back-breaking work, but the plastic sledge with its burden was moving, sliding slowly over the packed snow. Amos' arms and legs dangled over the edges, trailing along in the snow. Floss ran round and round them as they moved, barking and chivvying them as though she were driving sheep, bringing them in, herding them home. Inch by inch, they made the slow, tortuous journey to the back door of the house.

Rob felt that his arms and back and legs would surely give way from the aching strain by the time they reached it. His breath came in shuddering gasps and he was trembling violently. But they were within reach of the porch at last. A couple more heaves, and the red plastic sledge slid over the snowy doorway and came to a jarring, bone-shaking halt on the flagstones of the kitchen.

16

Rescue?

Rob kicked the door to behind him and stood for a moment, bent and gasping for breath, as he recovered from his efforts. The next thing he did was to stir into life the grey embers of the fire and throw on the last two logs from the pile beside it. Then he turned his attention to the sick old man on the floor.

Floss shook her coat free of the last clinging snowflakes and flopped with a groan upon the hearthrug, content now that all were safely indoors. Rob pulled off the woollen balaclava and heavy woollen gloves worn by Amos, undid the buttons on the Army coat and loosened the shirt collar underneath. The old man was still unconscious, his skin cold and grey, his breathing faint and irregular. Rob had done one or two First Aid sessions at school and wished he had done more. He racked his brains to try and remember what was the correct thing to do in these circumstances.

He rubbed at Amos' still, cold hands for a moment or two, then noticed the brandy bottle on the cluttered dresser. That was the thing to revive lambs who were 'starved', and maybe it would work for humans too. Wasn't it brandy that St Bernards carried in little kegs round their necks when searching for buried avalanche victims?

He poured a spoonful and tipped it carefully between the old man's blue lips. Some of it dribbled down upon the grey stubble on his chin, but some went into his mouth, and then Rob was overjoyed to see the old man's throat muscles move as he swallowed. A moment later Amos coughed, spluttered, coughed again, and then his eyelids flickered open.

They closed again almost immediately. Rob bent and shook the bony old shoulder with a feeling of desperation. 'Amos! Amos!'

The watery eyes opened again, this time with an expression of recognition. 'Eh? What be going' on now, then?' His voice tailed off into a groan of pain, and one hand came up to clutch at his chest. 'Tablets. Get me tablets.'

'What tablets?' Rob asked urgently, but the old man's eyes were closed again and he didn't answer. Rob got up and began to rummage through the jumble of old farming papers, sheep medicine bottles, matchboxes, candle stubs and other assorted clutter on the dresser. No tablets. He opened the top drawer and found amidst cotton reels, batteries, seed catalogues and bits of string, a small bottle of pills with Amos' name on it. The directions on the label were blurred and the words danced in front of Rob's eyes when he tried to decipher them, but eventually he made out the words 'dissolve under tongue when required'.

He took a tablet from the bottle and pushed it into Amos' mouth. The effect was immediate and dramatic. In a few minutes the old man heaved a sigh, groaned and opened his eyes again, complaining of the hardness of the stone flags under him. Rob fetched a cushion to go under his head and a blanket to cover him. But in just another few minutes Amos, with Rob's help, had struggled up into a sitting position and was ruefully rasping his stubbly chin with one hand.

Rob held his breath. 'Are you feeling better?'

'Oh, aye. Me tablets always does the trick, when I has one of these turns. Angina, they calls it. But I'm all right with me tablets.'

'You shouldn't have gone out like that, in the cold.'

Amos cocked an eye at him. 'Maybe you're right. But I managed to get there and back all right, didn't I?'

Rob could see that Amos remembered nothing of his collapse in the snow, being buried and the desperate struggles that Rob had made to get him back inside. Maybe he'd tell him all about it later, but for the moment it didn't matter. He said, 'D'you think you could get up on the bed if I helped you? You're cold and you ought to get warm.'

'Aye. I could do with a warm and a bit of a sleep. I'm not as young as I was.'

With Rob's help he managed to heave himself up and on to the edge of the bed, where Rob helped him off with his boots and thick socks and the heavy coat. The kettle was boiling merrily by now, so he found two hot-water bottles and filled them and put them at Amos' feet in the bed, covering him warmly with blankets.

'Ah! That's better!' said the old man, who was beginning to look and sound much more normal by now. 'I'll have a bit of a sleep now, but mind you wake me when they comes looking for you. You're a real handy boy and I wants to tell your folks so.' His bushy eyebrows drew together in a frown. 'Funny, but I can't seem to remember was there any new lambs in the shed when I went to look. They must have been all right, though, because I was on my way back in, wasn't I, when I had my bit of a turn.'

He leaned back against the pillow, closing his eyes, but then opened them again. 'That there ewe in the corner'll need some feed and water, if you could see to it. I wish as I could remember about the others. Did I put the feed out in the troughs for 'em, or did I decide to leave it till later?'

'I'll go and look,' said Rob. 'Don't worry about it, Amos. I'll see to them all.'

'Ah! You be a good boy, real handy!'

The old man seemed to relax, and Rob thought he had dropped off to sleep. Then Amos said drowsily, with his eyes still closed, 'We're getting a bit low on firewood, too, if you could just bring in a few loads from the woodshed round the back.'

Rob felt sick and dazed with tiredness. He wanted nothing more than to collapse in a chair and let his shaking arms and legs recover. But there was more work to do first. He fed the ewe a measure of sheepnuts from the half full bag beside the pen and filled her pan with water. Then he made three trips to and from the lean-to woodshed at the back of the house, first having to clear the piled snow from the entrance. He stacked the wood in an untidy pile beside the hearth, noticing tiredly the lumps of melting snow that had fallen from his boots.

Outside, the world after the storm seemed wrapped in a cold white silence, nothing stirring on the ground or in the cold grey sky. The only movement was the fluttering of hungry sparrows in the snow-laden branches of the plum trees near the back door. Rob took the shovel and dug a path to the buildings where the pregnant ewes were housed. He saw at once that Amos had not reached them before his collapse, for their feed troughs were empty and they greeted him with eager bleating. Two more lambs had been born during the night, both strong and well, on their feet and suckling.

Rob fetched a hay bale from the fodder store at the end of the barn, cut the strings, shook out the hay and spread it in the hay racks. He poured sheep-nuts into the feeding troughs, and was immediately surrounded by a mass of pushing, jostling, eager woolly bodies and munching jaws. He found a water tap and filled the long galvanized trough along the end of the building.

From their enclosure at the other end, the sheep-dogs were whining and yelping, eager to be let out for their day's work and exercise. Through a daze of weariness, Rob filled their water dishes and found a packet of dog food on a high shelf. They crowded around him in the doorway, pleading to be let out into the snow, but he had to close the door in their faces.

He could not be responsible for dogs whose master was not there to control them, and he had more sense than to try.

Besides, he was so tired that he could hardly stand upon his legs. He staggered a little as he walked back to the farmhouse.

He found old Amos asleep, breathing regularly and with a healthier tinge of colour upon his cheeks. Rob thought that he should have something warm to eat when he woke, but that would have to wait. The room was warm and the ewe munched contentedly with her twins beside her. By rights she should be joining the others, in the outbuildings, but that would have to wait too.

Everything would have to wait, because he was so exhausted that he could hardly move or speak or think. He dragged off his boots and his damp jacket, took a spare blanket and curled up in Amos' big chair with his head on an overstuffed cushion.

Neither of them was awake to hear when, halfway through the morning, a helicopter came whirring and clattering over the snowbound mountain, pausing and circling lower to take a look at the isolated farmhouse. The pilot saw a calm and peaceful scene below, smoke rising in a blue plume from the chimney showing that the occupants were alive and well. The helicopter circled once more and then gained height, turned and disappeared over the hill into the next valley.

17

Sacrifice

When morning came, a bright white light reflected from the snow filled the cave, showing up the huddled sheep at the far end, the dying fire, the haggard faces of the boy and girl. The blizzard had passed, and sunshine made a myriad shining points of light on the blanket of whiteness.

The wolves were still there.

This was Rac's first thought, as he opened his eyes after a half doze. There was a rough-coated grey shape in the snow a few feet beyond the cave's entrance, and another, and another. Just lying there, waiting.

He turned to Bara, to find her wide awake with her large dark eyes upon him. 'They are hungry,' she said. 'They know there's food here.'

'I was sure they'd go away when daylight came,' he replied, sick with dismay and apprehension.

The last piece of wood had been thrown upon the fire, and now it had died to a heap of smouldering ash, sifting out across the snow. 'We have no more wood,' Rac said.

They looked at each other without speaking.

'Suppose,' said Rac, 'suppose we threw out our food to them. Would they go away then?'

Bara shook her head. 'I don't think so. It's not enough. It would just make them want more.'

She turned her head quickly, but not before he saw a tear slide down her cheek. He reached for her hand.

'If they attack, I have my good strong spear. And we have the bow and some arrows. Maybe we can be strong enough.'

'Maybe.' She brushed the tear away from her cheek and said, 'I'm sorry, Rac. It's my fault we came away. It was my idea. You did it for me.'

Rac gave her hand a squeeze. 'And I would do it again,' he said.

They fell silent, sitting side by side.

At last Bara said, 'We should give the sheep a drink.' She took one of the cooking pots and poured water from the skin bags into it. Watching the way the sheep so trustingly accepted drink from her hands, even with danger lurking a stone's throw away, Rac was smitten to the heart again. They were all so soft and helpless and trusting, Bara and the sheep, and he longed to take care of them. But in this situation he was helpless too.

They had no heart for food but each took a drink themselves. The wolves lay watchfully, their yellow eyes sometimes half closed against the bright glare of sun reflected from snow, but opening again at the least movement from inside the cave. Rac felt that they would make no move during daylight hours. But night would come again, and this time there would be no fire.

They sat down, close together, with their backs against the rocky wall. Rac had his spear in his hand and Bara had the bow with arrows at the ready, but both felt secretly that these puny weapons would be a poor defence against a hungry pack.

'You can sleep a little, if you wish,' said Rac. 'I will keep watch.'

Bara did sleep for a while with her head on his shoulder, making little sobbing sounds in her sleep. She woke again when the Fire-in-the-Sky was going down, sending long blue shadows across the snow outside. The wolves were still there. The sheep were quiet. They had not eaten all day, but stayed motionless in the back of the cave, their eyes gleaming.

'You sleep for a while now,' said Bara, pushing back her hair with a gesture of weariness. 'It's a long time since you slept.'

'I do not feel the need,' said Rac stoutly.

But sleep he did, slumping sideways against the wall with his hand on the ash haft of his spear.

He awoke to a terrible commotion all around him, the terrified bleatings of sheep, a ferocious snarling and snapping of cruel teeth and then a shrill high scream that froze his blood. He was on his feet before his head cleared properly. He seized the spear, his eyes darting to the entrance of the cave and back again to see what had happened.

It was growing dark outside, Fire-Down was almost here, and the sun hung in a deep red ball on the horizon, clearly visible from the cave mouth. The sheep huddled and pressed together, panting and with staring eyes, as though they would push their woolly bodies into the rock walls with the strength of their fear. The fire was just a heap of dead ash.

The wolves had gone, and so had Bara.

Rac sprang from the cave, his eyes searching the snow-covered slopes, his spear poised to throw. His heart thudded painfully against his ribs. In front of the cave and for a distance around, the snow was trodden and disturbed, as though a tremendous struggle had taken place.

And there was blood. Deep crimson splashes and daubs staining the snow where the struggle had been, drops and spots and drips leading away across the hillside to disappear over a small rise.

Rac flung back his head and roared in anguish, running to and fro in the snow, floundering and stumbling and doubling back on himself, hardly knowing what he was doing.

And then he saw Bara, crouching in the snow beside a snow-covered rock not far away. Blood splattered her hair and her face and her deerskin tunic, and she was sobbing brokenheartedly into her blood-stained hands. But she was alive.

Rac covered the ground in two bounds. 'Bara! Are you hurt? Where? Let me see!'

She raised her face, stained with blood and tears, to him and sobbed harder for a moment. Then she said, 'I am not hurt. And the wolves have gone.'

'But—this blood—so much blood! Where has it come from?'

'From—from my lamb! My little one, my little pet ewe-lamb! They have taken her!' She sobbed again in a frenzy of pain and loss.

Rac knelt beside her in the snow. 'But how did it happen? Did the wolves come into the cave?'

She shook her head. 'No. They just went on waiting. There were only three, an old pair and another with a crippled hind leg. They must have been turned out from their pack because they could not keep up in the chase. That is the way with wolves. They were very hungry.'

'Then did the lamb run outside?'

The tears flowed afresh. 'No! You know how she was, she trusted me and would never leave my side.'

'Then what happened? I don't understand.'

Bara did not answer for a moment, her head turned away. Then she said, so softly that he had to bend close to hear, 'It was on my account that you came away. You would have died because of me. I thought—I thought, that maybe there was a way you could go free after all. If I—if I went out to the wolves, and they took me, they might have been satisfied and gone away, and left you and the sheep to live.'

Rac pressed his hands to his ears in horror. He could hardly believe what he was hearing. He said stupidly, 'But—but we came away because you were to be sacrificed. This would have been a sacrifice just the same.'

'There would have been a difference.'

'What difference?'

'I would have done it willingly.'

Rac's head was reeling. Why should Bara flee from one sacrifice only to offer herself as another? The answer came suddenly as he struggled to make sense of it all. Bara had done it because she cared for him. The knowledge was almost too much for him to grasp. He dropped his head into his hands and bent his face to his knees, overwhelmed by the thought. It had not been the way of his people to show love to one another.

Then another thought came. 'But you are alive. They did not kill you. And what is all this blood?'

Bara said forlornly, 'I had forgotten my lamb. That she would follow wherever I go. I waited until you slept and then I slipped out. She came after me. The wolves fell upon her at once and tore her to pieces in front of me. There was nothing left of her, except the blood. Then they went away. It was the sheep they wanted, not us.'

She put her head down on her knees in the same way as Rac, and they rocked side by side in shared horror, and grief, and finally relief.

It was Bara who recovered first. She raised her head and said, 'We still have the other sheep to care for. They have had no food today. Maybe we can find some vegetation if we dig under the snow. And we must eat, ourselves, and build a fire, and then sleep. There's only another day's journey to the pass. We could reach there tomorrow.'

Rac felt slow and stupid. 'Shall we go on, then? To find the new place?'

Bara was climbing to her feet. 'Yes. We can get wood and make a fire, but I don't think the wolves will come back tonight. They'll sleep for a stretch now that they've eaten. Get up, Rac. You look so stupid when you blink like that. It's all right. The lamb has died, but it means that we can go free.'

She smiled suddenly through the blood and the tears, and he felt life and hope flood through his whole being. He climbed to his feet and they walked back to the cave hand in hand.

Before they slept, Rac was suddenly aware again of the Presence, so strongly that it seemed as though the cold dark cave was flooded with light and warmth. They and the sheep slept soundly until dawn broke again.

There was a little food left in their packs. They gave the last barley cakes to the sheep and ate the strips of meat themselves, drank from the dewpond, took a look at the snowbound mountainside and began the long climb to the pass between the high peaks. No new wolf tracks showed in the snow, though there was plenty of the spoor of smaller creatures—foxes, rabbits, weasels—criss-crossing the pristine whiteness.

They were well above the snowline and could see brown earth and green growth on the lower slopes, where the storm would have fallen as rain and hail. Rac glanced briefly again at the dark mass of the oak forest, beyond which their villages lay. But they resolutely turned their backs upon it and climbed upward through the snow.

It took them almost all that day to reach the pass and it was again late afternoon when they came to the last long slope. The sheep were tired too, walking with hanging heads and panting breath, disliking the cold wetness reaching halfway up their sturdy legs. But suddenly there it was, an open gap between the mountains, with sky and clouds beyond.

Bara reached the brow first, with a sudden burst of fresh energy, springing up as nimbly as one of her lambs, eagerly scanning the scene before her and turning to laugh triumphantly down at him.

'This is it! Come and look!'

Rac joined her, panting with exertion. What he saw took away what remaining breath he had. Before him lay a beautiful valley, the snow of its upper slopes giving place to land still clothed with the colours of autumn, bronze and yellow and ochre and every shade of green, stretching away to faint blue hills in the distance, snow-capped like their own. There were wide stretches of green grass interspersed with woods of oak and ash, hazel and hawthorn and beech, wild apple and cherry, cover for deer and pig and rabbit and all kinds of game. Through the length of the valley a wide river curved and meandered, glinting silver in the last of the daylight.

'Water!' said Bara. 'Fish! Game! Berries and fruits. Wood for fires and for shelter. And plenty of grass for sheep. Everything we need.'

Rac's eyes surveyed the quiet autumn scene. There was everything that they would need for the coming Cold Time. And when the Warm Time came again it would be even more beautiful, clothed with fresh green and teeming with young wild life.

'No smoke anywhere,' he said. 'Does that mean no people?'

'I don't know,' Bara shook her head. 'That we will find out. Maybe we will be the first people here.'

Rac turned to look at her. 'Are you afraid?'

She thought for a moment. 'No. I was afraid, afraid of the others in my village, afraid of the wolves. But not any more. We will always take care of each other. And, the Other—the Great Spirit, whoever he is—he will take care of both of us.'

All of a sudden Rac felt again the Presence that had been with them in the cave last night, strong and wonderful and all-loving, standing there beside them looking at the new place. He could almost fancy that he heard a great Voice say, 'Do not fear. Go forward bravely, for I am with you.'

But he did not quite dare to say this yet, even to Bara. Instead, he said, 'When we find our place, I will scratch a new picture. The best I ever made.'

Bara smiled and squeezed his hand. He knew that she felt the Presence too. He said, knowing that she would understand perfectly, 'I wish that we could see him. Or know his name.'

Bara said rather wistfully, 'Maybe one day we will. Or if not us, then our children. Or theirs.'

The lambs were frisking ahead, kicking up the snow and tossing their heads, as though they too were suddenly refreshed by the prospect before them. There were only three of them now, but Rac's lamb had been totally accepted by the other two, the three of them banding together into a little flock, forgetting their differences. Green grass was somewhere ahead, they were young and hopeful, and their shepherds were close at hand.

'Let's go,' said Rac. The future beckoned, and there was much to be done. For tonight they must find safe shelter and wood for their fire. The dangers would be just as real in the new place, he knew, perhaps more if there were no other people. He could not tell what might be in store for them. But whatever came, they would face it together.

Next Fire-Rise would be the start of their new life, and there would be little time for looking back at the old. Hands still clasped, he and Bara followed the sheep down into the beautiful green valley.

18

HELP

Amos' pocket watch ticked away the hours of the morning, and it was almost one o'clock when the old man woke with a grunt and a clearing of the throat, startling Rob from his own deep sleep. Rob awoke slowly, reluctantly, blinking, with a feeling that was almost disappointment to find himself still in the stuffy farmhouse at Ty Mynydd. His heart was full of a kind of deep longing, to know where Rac and Bara had built their first home, how they had survived the winter, whether they had been happy in their new place. But instinctively he felt that the dreaming was done. He would never know. He heaved a deep sigh, and flung off the blanket.

'How are you, Amos?' he asked, turning to the old man in the bed.

'Oh, fair, boy, fair. I'll be right as rain when I've got summat in my belly.' He struggled up in the bed and began to fumble with the bedclothes.

Rob was already putting the kettle on to boil and puffing up the fire with the old bellows. 'You rest there a bit, Amos. I'll get some food. Just tell me where things are.'

Amos sank back against the pillows, relieved. 'I do feel a bit middlin' still. Good job you're here. Well, bless me, it's near on one o'clock! Half the day gone already! Put the wireless on, will you, and let's hear the forecast. You never know, there might be one of them police messages on the local news about you goin' missing.'

Rob's heart gave a jump. He had completely forgotten his own situation, forgotten that by now his parents must be almost frantic with worry about him, almost forgotten that he had a life outside this snowbound sheep-farm. He switched on the radio with some reluctance. For quite some while now he had feared and avoided news bulletins, especially in times of conflict, and the habit had stuck. While the newsreader droned on depressingly of recession and inflation, he found saucepans and tinned stew and fruit and potatoes in the adjoining pantry.

While the food heated, he took a peep into the small sitting-room next door, the 'parlour', as Amos called it. It was neat but chilly, with heavy oak furniture and chairs under covers, evidently seldom if ever used. Rob went up the narrow steep stairs with a bend in them and looked at the two bedrooms, each with its faded patterned carpet, old-fashioned washstand complete with jug and basin, and large oak beds, also covered by dustsheets. That was all there was of the house, and it was plain that all the living and cooking and eating and resting went on in the cluttered kitchen.

They ate their meal from large chipped plates and drank strong tea with powdered milk. Amos explained that a neighbour usually brought two pints of milk, twice a week. 'But I won't see him for a day or two, I don't suppose, with a fall like this.' After the meal, Amos announced his intention of getting up and going about his business, but was alarmed to find returning pain when he tried to rise. He sat on the edge of the bed, his hand to his chest, and asked Rob to pass the tablets.

'Must have been a baddish turn I had,' he said worriedly. 'It's knocked me about a bit. By rights I ought to be out after the sheep, but I don't know as I can. It was a lot easier the way folks did things years ago, with the sheep-place right next to the kitchen and a door opening through.'

Rob could see that there might be something to be said for the old Welsh long-houses, in weather like this. He persuaded Amos to get back into bed and fetched his tablets. He cleared the dishes and piled them into the stone sink, fed the dog, and between them he and Floss shepherded the ewe with the twins out of the kitchen and across to join the others. While he was there, he checked the ewes and found a new set of triplets, one of whom seemed smaller and weaker than the others and unable to feed from its mother. He brought it inside and put it into the pen the ewe had occupied.

Amos was feeling a bit better by now and told him where to find the milk substitute powder he used for weak lambs and gave him directions on how to mix it.

He watched while Rob tried to feed the lamb, which was both weak and obstinate at the same time, refusing at first to suckle, clamping its teeth tightly shut so that the milk dribbled uselessly down its chin.

'Stubborn lambs is the very dickens,' observed old Amos gloomily from his bed, and Rob was inclined to agree.

He was still struggling with the lamb when a mechanical clattering sounded from outside. 'A helicopter!' said Amos, who had heard the sound in other winters. 'Quick, boy, get out there and wave! Let 'em know you're here.'

Rob dumped the lamb and made for the door. But the pilot was giving no more than a casual glance at Ty Mynydd this time, and before Rob could emerge the helicopter was already past, growing smaller and smaller against the grey sky.

He returned, crestfallen, to the kitchen. Amos took one look at his glum face. 'They'll be back, boy. They'll keep looking till they finds you, never fret!'

'I was too slow,' said Rob. 'What we need is some kind of signal.'

He thought about it while he worked over the lamb, finally getting it to suck and swallow properly. A fire, perhaps, out of doors with plenty of smoke? But it would take an awful lot of work and fuel to build and maintain a large enough one, and who could tell how long he might have to keep it going? He abandoned that idea. A white flag, maybe, tied on some high point? No, white would be no good against a background of snow. It would have to be some bright colour.

The red plastic mineral supplement bags—that was it! He could arrange them in the snow to spell out a message, for next time the helicopter came. Hopefully there would be a next time. Anyway, it was worth a try.

By the time the lamb finished the bottle, Amos was dozing again. Rob pulled on his jacket and boots and gathered together the stack of empty red plastic bags and carried them out into the snow. He'd have to find a smooth flat place that would show up from the air. The snowy scene was quite breathtaking, drifts and mounds and great waves of it stretching as far as he could see under a sullen grey sky, with the vast white peaks of the mountain looming over all. Here at Ty Mynydd they were out of view of any other habitation, tucked away in a fold of the hills. It might have been the last place on earth.

Above the farmhouse he came to a flat, unbroken stretch of snow, a distance away from the huddle of farm buildings. Breath streaming white in the cold air, he began to spell out his message.

He hoped there would be enough of the red bags to last out. Three for the downstroke of the H, one for the bar across the middle, three for the other side. That was simple. Then the E with one bag folded under a little to make the shorter middle bar, then an L which was easy too. The P presented a few difficulties, with its rounded loop in front but he arranged the bags as best he could. The P's loop was a bit square-looking, but he was satisfied that the whole thing spelt out his message clear and plain, in large red letters against the white snow. The wind had dropped completely and he'd filled his pockets with a few stones from around the doorways of the sheep pen to anchor the bags with, and hoped they'd be enough to hold.

He was sweating by the time he'd finished, but checked the sheep again before he went in, taking with him an armful of wood for the fire. Now all they had to do was wait.

19

Rob's secret

The afternoon seemed very long. As the day passed the old man grew increasingly grumpy and morose, fretting to be out and about with his sheep but knowing that he dare not take the risk. Rob made tea and heated food. He had still not got round to washing up yet, telling himself he would do it all in one go a little later. He checked the ewes, let the young dogs out for a short run (though he had some difficulty rounding them up again) and fed the 'tiddler' lamb at intervals. It was very still out of doors, and he hoped the strong wind wouldn't return and blow the red bags about. He kept the fire going, fetched in firewood and chopped more. And waited.

He had no doubt at all that he would eventually be rescued. But another thought had been troubling him increasingly as the afternoon wore on. What would happen to the old man when he himself was found and taken home?

Sitting by the fire opposite Amos, he tentatively broached the question. Amos was ensconced in his dilapidated armchair. He was dozing.

'Amos, who's going to see to the lambing when I've gone?'

The old man's bushy eyebrows came together in a frown. 'What's that? Well, who d'you think? How d'you think I managed before you dropped by? Eh?'

He sounded so cross that Rob hesitated to mention the recent 'turn'. He was sure that even now Amos didn't realize how ill he had really been. Or maybe he just wouldn't admit to it. At any rate, Rob was sure that going out into the cold and doing the hard and rigorous shepherding work would prove too much for the old man. He might even die, all alone in the snow and cold, without even the help of a puny thirteen-year-old boy.

He tried again. 'Wouldn't it be a good idea to go down to the town with me and see a doctor or something?'

'What? And get stuck into some 'ospital? You never comes out of them places alive! Or if you do, you're sure to pick up something or other, with all them sick people about! They might want to put me into one of them old folks homes. And what'd happen to my sheep then? No, I'll stop here until they carries me out in a box!'

Rob felt a twinge of sympathy. To be confined to a centrally-heated, sedentary, sheltered environment would surely seem like a living death to someone who had spent eighty years or more on the open mountainside, independent and battling the elements, summer and winter alike. And the sheep. The sheep were Amos' whole life, his reason for living.

There seemed no answer to the problem, so he gave up thinking about it.

Instead, his mind turned to Mum and Dad and home. Amos' diet of porridge and powdered milk and potatoes and tinned stuff was getting a bit monotonous. He could do with a nice plate of fish and chips, or one of Mum's apple crumbles with ice cream, or macaroni cheese, or a Chinese takeaway... He sighed, and said, 'Shall I make you a cup of tea, Amos?'

'If you wants to.'

Rob put the kettle on and stoked up the fire, suddenly feeling very depressed himself. What was it all for, anyway? What was the point of Amos' existence if he was only going to end up ill and alone and fearful?

He jumped a little when Amos said suddenly, 'Mind you, I'm not grumbling. I reckon I've had a good innings—a happy life down here and a long 'un. I'm about ready to go on to the next, I reckon.'

Rob felt uncomfortable. Amos almost seemed to read his mind sometimes. He felt even more uncomfortable when Amos suddenly sat up straighter, took the mug of tea Rob handed him and said, 'You was just going to tell me all about your brother, wasn't you, before that ewe started to lamb.'

Rob's heart sank like a stone. For a while, with everything that had happened, he'd forgotten all about Nick and the constant guilt that he'd carried for what seemed a very long time. He was tempted to pretend he'd forgotten all about the previous conversation. But

Amos' eye was on him and Amos was no fool.

He said, 'Nick's away. He's stationed in Germany at the moment. I haven't seen him for a long time.'

Amos' eyebrows lifted. 'Was he in that there Gulf War?'

Rob felt the familiar clutch of fear at his insides. He said very quietly, 'Yes.'

'But he came through all right?'

'Yes. But—'

'But what?'

'But there's still fighting in other places. He goes all over the place. And—and—sometimes I think he'll never come back.'

'Why's that, then?'

Rob took a deep breath, 'Because I don't deserve it. Before he went away, I did something terrible. I nearly killed him.' And suddenly it was all pouring out, the sad story that he had held inside himself for so long, rushing and tumbling and breaking free in a jumble of words.

'We had an argument, sort of. He was on leave, and he had a brand new scrambler bike, a Kawasaki. I could have handled it all right. But he wouldn't even let me try. He and Pete went scrambling every day that leave, and I couldn't even have one go. Not even one.'

Tears came back at the injustice of it. The memory of watching his brothers handle the big powerful machines, bucking, wheeling, roaring, cornering, the smell of diesel oil and dust and hot fumes thick and exciting in the air. And himself just watching, as usual, from the sidelines, having no real part in it. The baby brother always too young to be included.

He said, choking a little, 'They never even thought of letting me join in. It was always the same. I asked Nick again, nicely, to let me have just one go on the Kawasaki. Sometimes he let me do things if I asked him nicely. And he just laughed at me, and swerved round and kicked up a lot of dust in my face.'

Amos heaved a sigh. 'Well, that's the ways of young boys. Not much thought for the feelin's of others. That comes with age. I daresay you was upset, wasn't you?'

'I was mad. Hopping mad. I wanted to get back at him. He and Pete never let me do anything. Just because Mum made a bit of a fuss and thought I was too small. She'd never have known.'

'Her'd have known all right if you'd come to grief.'

'I wouldn't have. I can ride as well as they can.' He paused, and then went on in a rush, 'Anyway, that same evening, when Nick had gone out with his friends, I went out and cut the brake cables on his new bike.'

He paused again, holding his breath. It was out. His dreadful deed was confessed.

Amos was gazing keenly at him. 'And he met with an accident, did he, your brother?'

Rob shook his head. 'Oh no. He didn't ride the bike again. In any case, I told my other brother, Pete, what I'd done, that same night. He thumped me good and hard and told me I was a little fool.'

Amos nodded. 'Quite right too. Well then?' The old man took a sip of his tea, his expression alert and his recent depression quite forgotten.

'Well, Pete told me I'd better keep quiet about it if I knew what was good for me. If Nick found out he'd thump me even harder and serve me right too. But I thought I'd better own up. I was going to. But I never saw Nick again. He got called up to go to the Gulf, and he was gone before I got up the next morning. Pete fixed the bike for me, and Mum and Dad never knew anything about it.'

He gulped back a sob or two. 'It—it was awful when the Gulf War was on. Every day I was afraid there'd be something on the news. He was in the desert, seconded to the Desert Rats. They were in the front line.'

It was still painful to talk about. At the time, all the boys at school had thought Nick was a hero, and kept asking questions. He'd lost some friends because he wouldn't talk about it. Mum and Dad had prayed, and so had everyone at their church.

He'd prayed, too, in the very beginning, desperately and often. If Nick died in the war it would be all his fault, because he had done something on purpose that could have killed his brother.

The Gulf War had ended, and there was great rejoicing. Young soldiers and airmen were coming home to welcoming banners, balloons, parties, celebrations. But not Nick. Nick had decided to go on a trip to the Greek Islands with some friends instead, and then back to his base in Germany. They'd had letters and a long cheerful phone call saying he might be posted back to Britain before long and that he'd see them all then. Mum and Dad had taken a weekend flight to Germany to see him, and came back with reports that he was fine, which made them all feel much happier. But Rob hadn't seen Nick at all. Deep down, he didn't believe he would, somehow. Ever.

He was in tears by the time he got to this part of the story. Amos leaned forward. 'What makes you say that, then?'

Rob put his head in his hands and sobbed. 'Can't you see? God isn't going to let him come back because of what I did. He's punishing me for it. I won't ever see Nick again, because I don't deserve to.'

'Here, here now. Hold up a bit. I reckon you're wrong there. Your brother was about right when he said you'd been a silly fool. But that's about it. It was all done in a bit of a temper-paddy, but no harm done. You can't go blaming yourself for everything else as well. You'm taking too much on yourself. Too heavy a load.'

Rob gulped. The load he carried was heavy indeed.

The old man was silent for a moment, deep in thought. Then he said, 'There's summat in the Bible about heavy loads. I'm wondering can I remember how it goes.'

Rob felt his heart begin to close in self-defence. He'd finished with God, and he didn't want to hear if Amos was going to start quoting Bible passages at him. God didn't want to know, and he didn't want to know God.

But suddenly he remembered the desperate cry for help he'd made, out there in the blizzard with Amos lying half-buried and helpless. Had it been God who'd helped him then?

Amos was reciting, 'Come unto me all ye who labour and are heavy laden, and I will give you rest. Take my yoke upon you and learn of me, for I am meek and lowly in heart and you shall find rest unto your souls. For my yoke is easy and my burden is light.' He stopped, looking pleased with himself. He seemed to have quite forgotten his own earlier despondency. 'Word-perfect, nearly. I was always good at memorizing Scriptures. Them's good words. What do you think?'

Rob nodded. At home and in their own church they used a modern version of the Bible, but there was something very impressive about the old language.

'I reckon,' said Amos slowly, 'I reckon you've got a bit of a wrong idea about God. That's my opinion, for what it's worth. Somewhere along the line you've picked up some wrong notions. What would you say God is like, if I was to ask you?'

Rob felt uncomfortable. He thought of all the obvious things like 'God is love' and, 'In the beginning God created—', the things he'd heard preached Sunday after Sunday. He sighed and gave up. 'I don't really know what he's like.'

'Well then, I'll tell you. Listen to this. Jesus said: "I am the good shepherd: the good shepherd giveth his life for the sheep. But he that is an hireling, and not the shepherd, whose own the sheep are not, seeth the wolf coming, and leaveth the sheep, and fleeth: and the wolf catcheth them, and scattereth the sheep. The hireling fleeth, because he is an hireling, and careth not for the sheep. I am the good shepherd, and know my sheep, and are known of mine. As the Father knoweth me, even so know I the Father, and I lay down my life for the sheep. And other sheep I have, which are not of this fold: them also I must bring, and they shall hear my voice; and there shall be one fold, and one shepherd." John ten, eleven to sixteen.'

Rob had heard this read before, but somehow, here, recalled in the creaky voice of a sick old man in a stuffy, smelly farm kitchen with a lamb in the corner and more sheep just across the snowbound yard, it seemed different. This old man knew all about shepherding and the wayward, stupid, stubborn ways of sheep. Ewes wandered off and got lost, squeezed through hedges into forbidden and dangerous places, were obstinate and silly, following others where they shouldn't go. They could be easily fooled and deceived into believing things that were not true—just like people. But the shepherd never ever punished them or stopped loving and caring for them.

'Now then,' said Amos. 'What is God like?'

'He's like a shepherd, like Jesus,' said Rob, and then, with a flash of revelation, 'He *is* Jesus.'

Suddenly, with this knowledge, the weight was lifted off his shoulders. He'd been wrong. God wouldn't pay him back for his stupidity, God cared, and loved, and forgave. Like Jesus, the good shepherd. His awful deed could be forgiven and forgotten.

A clattering mechanical sound disturbed the stillness of the darkening afternoon. The helicopter was returning at last, and this time it would not pass by, because the red plastic message on the hillside would be there to guide it.

20

The Sea King

Rob was on his feet in a moment, pulling on his jacket and his boots, slamming the porch door behind him as he ran out into the cold afternoon. This helicopter was a different one, much larger than the ones before, an RAF rescue Sea King. And it had seen his message! It circled like some huge bird of prey and came down into the smooth snow on that small plateau on the mountainside.

Rob began to run, gulping in great breaths of cold air, hardly looking where he was going, floundering into deep snow and out again, keeping his eyes on the huge chopper. He felt the strong draught from the giant propellers, saw the red plastic bags torn from their anchoring stones and blown and scattered like paper tissues over the hillside. But they had served their purpose. The helicopter had landed in the snow.

Rob slowed to a walk, completely out of breath, and saw two figures jump down from the doorway. The men, in bulky cold-weather clothes, were getting their bearings as they looked down at the huddle of farm buildings. Rob wasn't sure that they had seen him. He found more breath from somewhere, cupped his hands round his mouth and yelled at the top of his voice, 'Hey! Hey! Over here!'

Now they had both seen and heard him, waving and beginning to come towards him. One of them shouted back from between cupped hands, 'Hello! Are you Clive Roberts?'

'Yes!' shouted Rob, and held high his two arms with thumbs up. He waited for the men, suddenly shaky with excitement and relief. Rescue had come. His ordeal was over. He'd soon be home again and could leave behind the grimy, cluttered little place that was Amos' home, along with the hard work and the lack of comforts. He was looking forward to his comfortable bed, Mum's cooking, his computer, the telly.

The men reached him, breaking the unmarked snow with their long striding legs. Even though they were used to dramatic rescue operations, they couldn't disguise their own joy and relief at finding him safe and well. Not all rescues had such happy endings. They asked him a few brief questions, then one of them turned back to the Sea King to radio in immediately to HQ that Rob was alive and well.

The other man walked with Rob to the farmhouse where Amos waited. 'The old man all on his own, is he?' he asked.

Rob nodded. 'Yes. He hasn't been very well. I've been helping him. He's feeling better now though.'

'Right. I'll take a look at him. Maybe we ought to take him in as well if he's been ill.'

Amos had got to his feet to watch the helicopter landing from the window. He was still standing as they entered, the Sea King pilot greeting him cheerfully. Amos replied politely, but Rob saw at once that the old man's face was greyish again and that the effort of walking had caused a slight film of perspiration to break out on his forehead.

'Young Clive here says you've been unwell,' the pilot was saying, holding out his large hands to the fire's heat. 'What do you say to taking a ride in our chopper and going for a check?'

Amos replied by sitting down at once in his favourite armchair with his back to the door. 'No. That's what I say. I can't leave here. There's the sheep. Right in the middle of lambing, we are.' He glared accusingly at the young pilot, who smiled reassuringly and tried again.

'It wouldn't be for long, Mr Griffiths. Maybe just a few hours, or overnight. Then we'd fetch you back.'

Rob could see that Amos had quickly decided to be at his most stubborn. 'No. I'm stopping here. You take this young lad back to his folks and leave me be. I've got me tablets, and I'll be all right.'

The pilot sighed. 'Well, if you won't come, you won't. Maybe a doctor will be able to come out and take a look at you. You really should see someone.'

'They can please theirselves.' Amos' lips were set in a thin obstinate line. 'But I'm not budging from here.'

He and the pilot eyed each other for a moment and then the pilot gave up. He'd dealt with many stubborn people in his time, refusing to leave flooded houses, or friends in danger, or sick relatives, but he knew when he was beaten. He said, 'Well, all right then. Now then, young lad, are you ready for the off? I bet your Mum'll be glad to see you in one piece.'

The lamb bleated shrilly from the pen in the corner as Rob searched around for his few belongings, the crash helmet and his second pair of socks. He hesitated. It was time to feed the lamb again. He wondered if the helicopter men would wait while he mixed a bottle and fed it, to save Amos the fiddly, time-consuming task. Then it was almost time for the evening rounds of the sheep shed, the watering and feeding and littering, not to mention looking out for any new lambs. The dogs were barking furiously, driven to a frenzy by the sounds of a strange machine and strange men. They would need feeding too.

He stopped in the middle of pulling on a sock, realization dawning with slow certainty.

Amos just couldn't manage on his own, even for one night.

There was no one else.

He would have to stay.

He sighed, and abandoned thoughts of a good hot bath, his electric blanket, sausage and chips, his favourite Motocross programme, not to mention the prospect of being in the limelight for once and showing off a little.

It would all have to wait. He looked at the Sea King pilot and said, 'I'm not going either. Not tonight. Not until someone's here to help him.'

By the time the other RAF man had come in from radioing the good news to Rob's family, the pilot had given in again. In the end they agreed to leave Rob there for one more night, after which other arrangements could hopefully be made. They checked supplies at the house, foodstuffs, fuel and medical, and gave Rob some chocolate and dried fruit from their emergency supplies. Rob wrote a note on the back of an old calendar and gave it to them for Mum, explaining the situation as he saw it. Then they left before dusk fell.

Walking back through the deep snow to the chopper, the pilot shook his head. 'I've met some stubborn folk in my time, but, young or old, these border people take some beating!'

21

Together again

The second night passed peacefully, with Amos snoring gently in his bed, and Rob on an old mattress from the cupboard under the stairs. It was flock-filled, hard and lumpy, but better than an armchair, and he slept well.

He set the alarm for three and got up to check the ewes, going out with Floss into a still, frosty night, piercingly cold, with a myriad points of icy brilliance glistening and dancing in the torch beam. All was quiet in the lambing shed, and he returned to bank up the fire and fall at once into a sound and dreamless sleep.

In the morning Amos was awake first. He had boiled the kettle and was stirring porridge for breakfast by the time Rob woke. Rob could see at once that the old man was much better. The way he moved about, the colour in his cheeks, even the firmer tone of his voice, all spoke of returning strength.

After a hard frost, sunshine was streaming in through the kitchen window, flooding the cluttered room with bright white light. Rob pulled back the blankets and rolled out of his makeshift bed. He felt chirpy and light-hearted and very hungry. Even the bubbling porridge smelled appetizing, and when Amos produced some bacon from somewhere and began to fry rashers in a pan, Rob felt that his cup of happiness was full.

Before eating, however, he knew he that he had to check the livestock and see to their breakfasts. It was a busy morning. In the way that ewes have, several decided to give birth all at once. There were no real complications, but he was kept fully occupied for some time checking on the new arrivals, making sure first that they breathed and a little later got up to suckle on spindly, wobbling legs. New mothers were dosed and watered, the rest fed and fresh litter spread for all.

Amos stayed indoors, seemingly content to see to the housekeeping and let Rob do the outdoor work. He seemed pleased with events in general, though he had tried to persuade Rob to go home the day before. At lunchtime he produced a tin of chocolate biscuits, unopened, a Christmas gift from a neighbour, and pressed Rob to help himself. Feet toasting on the fender and pleasantly relaxed after the morning's work, Rob was glad to oblige.

He had half-forgotten that the Sea King would be coming back to pick him up that day. It was already early afternoon when he heard the clattering that heralded its approach. He had been exercising the young sheepdogs, watching them run and roll and flounder joyfully in the snowdrifts. He quickly gathered them together and shut them in again with a handful of dog biscuits as the chopper appeared over the hill.

Rob stood and watched the Sea King land in the same place as before, squinting against the bright rays of the sun. Figures began to emerge, more than before, three, four, five! Three tall young men, one older, slightly shorter and broader, and a woman. Rob would have known the woman anywhere, even dressed as she was in the unfamiliar ski-suit, because it was his mum.

He let out a yell and began to run, stumbled into a deep drift, fell, threshed about for a moment, scrambled to his feet and struggled on. Mum was running too, her woolly hat falling off and lying forgotten on the snow, her mouth calling his name, although he couldn't hear the sound of it. They met breathless halfway between the farmhouse and the Sea King, at the edge of Amos' little orchard full of wind-stunted snow-laden apple trees.

Mum's face was very red and her eyes bright. She said, 'Clive, oh, Clive!' but couldn't say anything else for a while, just held him tightly. Then she held him away and looked at him, peering closer and feeling his arms and shoulders and face to see if he was ill, or injured, or half-starved or frostbitten. Seeing that none of these things had happened to him, she said, 'Clive, it's freezing, and there you are with your jacket undone and nothing on your head!'

Rob laughed. It was good to see Mum, good to hear her voice and even good to hear himself called Clive, which only Mum did these days, because a couple of years ago he'd decided that it was cissy.

Mum laughed too, their breaths mingling cloudy-white in the cold air. The others came up, and he saw with surprise that the older man was Dad.

'Dad!' he said. 'What are you doing here? Who's looking after the lambing and foddering and all that?'

Dad and Mum exchanged glances, as much as to say, 'There you are! He hasn't the faintest idea what we've been going through.'

But Dad only said, 'The neighbours are rallying round. It isn't every day a young lad goes missing in a snowstorm, thank goodness! We wanted to see why you wouldn't come home yesterday, and what was going on here. Are you OK?'

'Fine!' said Rob. 'I've been here all the time, helping Amos with the lambing.'

Dad's eyebrows went up, and he and Mum exchanged another glance. Dad gave him a mock punch on the chin. Then Rob saw that one of the young men was Pete, grinning under the Russian fur hat he wore in cold weather. He was impressed. Pete never missed a day's work for anything. His disappearance had made far more impact than he'd realized. All Pete said was, 'What have you done with the Quad, then?' but Rob could see that really it wasn't the Quad that mattered at all, it was him.

He was beginning to try to explain that the Quad was probably still well buried under the snowfall, when he noticed the other two young men.

One was the helicopter pilot who had come yesterday, tall and grinning.

The other was Nick!

Rob felt his jaw drop and the cold air rush into his mouth. He blinked, half disbelieving his own eyes. But it was Nick all right, relaxed and smiling, wearing the green ski-suit he'd got for the RAF skiing championships two years ago.

'Hi kid!' he said. 'What mess have you been getting into now, then?'

Rob couldn't answer. He felt a foolish grin spread over his face. The others began to discuss what they should do next. The first thing seemed to be to find Amos and discover the facts about his state of health.

They all made their way down the snowy slope to the farmhouse with its plume of blue smoke, the four men ahead and Mum and Rob bringing up the rear.

Rob's mind buzzed with questions. 'What's Nick doing here? It's not because I was missing, is it?'

Mum laughed, her mittened hand upon his shoulder as though she wanted to hold on to him now that she had him back. 'No, of course not! News travels fast, but not that fast! Nick met up with us at Uncle Tom's funeral, quite unexpectedly. I'd wired to let him know, and he was able to come over in time. Good news, Clive. He's home on leave for a while, and after that he's being posted back to Britain. He travelled back from London with us.'

Rob was trying hard to take everything in. He asked, 'And is he staying in this country now? For good?'

'For a while at least. He's got a permanent ground posting. He's having a long leave first, though. It's good to have him back. But then for a while we thought we'd lost you—oh dear—'

Rob saw that she was suddenly close to tears. The last few days had been very hard on her. He reached up and gave her hand a squeeze. 'I was all right, Mum. Amos took care of me. And then I helped him.'

They were almost at the farmhouse with its square of faint yellow light at the window. Nick and the pilot went to have a look at the yard and outbuildings while the others headed for the house. Reminded of Amos, Rob said, 'Mum, I was wondering—could I stay with Amos for a bit longer? Just a week or two, for the lambing? He really is ill, you see. It's angina, or something. A few weeks off school wouldn't hurt—'

He was a little put out when both Dad and Pete burst out laughing, and Dad said, 'A nice try, son! But I don't think we're going to let you loose for a tidy while now!'

Mum said, 'Amos is really ill, then, is he?' but before he could answer they had reached the house and trooped into the porch.

When Rob lifted the latch he noticed the warm, stuffy, sheep-smelling air that met them from inside, but he couldn't quite understand the reactions of the others.

'Wow!' said Pete, clapping a hand over his nose. 'What a pong!'

'Oh dear,' said Mum, 'it is a bit smelly!' And when she saw the kitchen itself she looked both taken aback and dismayed. 'Oh, Clive. Have you been living in this?'

Rob looked around. He supposed the stuffy, crowded room, with its penned lamb, its sheep medicines and drying coats and damp socks, not to mention the piles of dirty dishes, saucepans and discarded food cans, would appear to be a bit of a tip to someone as fussy and particular as Mum. He hardly noticed the clutter any more, himself, even the sheepy smell seemed quite warm and companionable. But he saw his idea of staying with Amos for a while vanish into thin air. He wished he'd tidied up a bit, but it was too late now.

'Where is Amos?' asked Mum. And then she saw him, sitting in his armchair with its back to the doorway 'to keep back the draught' as he'd told Rob. Mum went over to him and took his hand and asked him how he was.

The old man blinked up at his visitors, a little tired after his morning's burst of activity. 'I'm fair to middling, thank you, Mrs Roberts. A cold old spell we're having. And how are your lambs coming, Mr Roberts?'

Somehow they were all sitting round the fire, talking of things like the weather, and the lambing, and all the kerfuffle there'd been when Rob was found to be missing, and how the area had already been combed unsuccessfully by other helicopters. Rob's family were favourably impressed by his idea of spelling out the help message with the red mineral bags.

Rob put on the kettle for more tea and then remembered that it was time to feed the lamb again.

Amidst all the excitement, one thought was uppermost in his mind. Nick was safe! He was here, out in the farmyard with the helicopter pilot, not a hundred yards away. It was taking him a time to adjust to the sheer unexpectedness of it all.

There were more surprises to come. They had just put the tea to brew in the pot and were searching for enough clean mugs when the door opened again, and in came Nick and the pilot on a blast of cold air, laughing and talking about technical aircraft things, stamping the snow from their boots, seeming to fill the already crowded kitchen.

Nick said, 'Brr! It's cold! I like a bit of Mediterranean sun myself. Almost forgot what Wales is like in the winter. Have you got a nice hot cup of tea there, kid?'

The pilot put his hand into his inner pocket and brought out a packet. 'Almost forgot. I've got some mail for you here, Mr Griffiths. A few days' worth, at least, I'd say.' He handed the letters to Amos. Rob looked at them—a few boring, buff-coloured ones of the type his Dad received, and a farming paper. There was another, an airmail letter with bright Australian stamps. Amos ignored the others and began to rummage for his reading glasses. 'Is it from Megan?' asked Rob.

'Clive!' said Mum. 'It's none of your business. Drink your tea and come and help me with the washing-up.'

Amos took quite a while over the reading of the letter, going over and over each page several times, nodding his head. The men drank their tea and drifted out again, to look at the stock and try to assess what kind of help Amos would need, and how they could get him to accept it. While they were about it they would do the evening rounds.

Mum and Rob tackled the dirty dishes together at the old stone sink, with a kettleful of hot water and washing soda. Amos had read the letter several times and appeared to have fallen into a doze with it still in his hands. Mum had inspected the cupboards, with a great deal of tut-tutting, and decided that she was going to make some pastry for a huge meat-and-vegetable pie, using tinned steak and vegetables, when they had cleared up a little. She had also found some disinfectant and washed down all the surfaces, putting things away where she thought they ought to belong. Rob wasn't happy about this at all. He was quite sure that Amos would never be able to find anything he needed again. But there was no stopping Mum when she got the bit between her teeth, that was what Dad always said. She would be washing socks and shirts and towels next, he thought, uneasily, all quite unnecessary things to do in his opinion.

He said, 'I wonder what's in the letter from Australia. Megan—that's Amos' daughter—is always trying to get Amos to go out to Australia to live, but he doesn't want to. He doesn't think much of Australian sheep stations. And it would be too hot for him there. He doesn't fancy the mosquitoes. Or the dust.'

Mum glanced at Amos, to make sure he was really dozing. Then she gave Rob a look, the kind of look that would have been over the top of her glasses if she'd been wearing them.

'You seem to know an awful lot about the situation.'

'Well, we talked a lot, most of that first night really. Except when the ewe was lambing. And when Amos had a bad turn and got buried and I had to dig him out.'

Mum gave him another look. 'Are you sure you're not exaggerating a bit? Amos never said anything about you digging him out of the snow. I know he's not very well, but I think you probably slept more than you realized.'

Rob sighed, wiping a plate and carefully stacking it with the others. No one ever gave him proper credit for anything, not even Mum. Not even after all that had happened. He'd been going to tell her about the arrowhead, and the dreams he'd had about the boy and girl of long ago, but decided he wouldn't after all. He wasn't quite sure whether they'd been dreams anyway, or his own imagination stirred up and stimulated by the blizzard and the strangeness and the disturbed night. He'd never forget them, though. He'd always wonder about them, and wish he knew if they'd found a place to live, and how they'd survived the winter, and how they'd fared with their sheep.

'I suppose we'll all have to stay the night, if the pilot agrees,' Mum was saying. 'I wonder if there's enough bedding. I don't suppose it'll be aired. Have you noticed any hot water bottles about? But how we're going to help Amos in the long term, I really don't know.'

From the sudden clearing of the throat from Amos' armchair, Rob had a suspicion that Amos had been awake and listening to their conversation all the time.

The old man leaned forward and said, 'Don't you go worrying about me, Mrs Roberts, thank you all the same. I had some good news in this here letter.' He held up the letter with the bright stamps. 'This letter should have reached me a week or more ago, by rights. My Megan's coming over to visit me, she says. The nineteenth. That's tomorrow. She'll have to drop in by helicopter, like you did, with the roads still closed.' He chuckled wheezily. 'So you see, you don't need to worry. I knew as it would all work out. Her'll put me to rights. My grandson might be coming too, the one in the Air Force. Only he's left now and wants to go sheep farming like his Dad. They'll fix up everything between them.'

Rob and his mother looked at each other. This news from Australia solved a great many problems in one go. Mum let out a sigh of relief. 'Oh, what a blessing! I couldn't for the life of me work out what we were going to do. I'm so glad. Go and call the men, Clive, and let's tell them the good news!'

Rob felt a strange twinge of regret that this night would definitely be the last he would spend at Ty Mynydd, though he was as glad as his mother that Amos would have someone to take care of him. In spite of everything, he had enjoyed the adventure. Returning to ordinary life and school would be something of an anticlimax.

The meal was prepared and eaten, the triplet lamb fed. It had given up being stubborn and nibbled eagerly at his hands when he picked it up. He put it down on the floor for a bit of exercise and it tottered after him when he went to fetch more wood from the porch.

The night had closed in, cutting off the little farm, marooned like an island in a sea of snow. Rob closed the door on the cold and carried an armful of wood through into the kitchen. Mum made coffee. The men stuck their long legs with feet in thick socks all round the fireplace. Looking round at their faces, red-tinged from the leaping flames, Rob felt the last trace of regret dissolve in a glow of inner warmth. Nick was home. He was safe. His own guilt feelings were gone, and he knew that they would never return.

His family was complete again, and tomorrow they would all go home.

Postscript:

March, Ty Mynydd

The snow had long gone, and already it was difficult to remember that freezing, bitter spell of wintry weather. The thaw had been followed by rain, floods, gales—and finally a dry spell with a keen south-east wind that was rapidly drying the sodden winter ground and ruffling the powdery yellow catkins on the hazels.

This morning the sun shone and patches of cloud were scudding across a grey-blue March sky. All week Dad had been busy ploughing and fertilizing and drilling seed for the next season's crops. Nick, still on leave, had been helping. Peter was back at work driving his huge truck to the docks at all hours of the day and night. Mum had begun her annual burst of spring cleaning and decorating. Rob was back at school. He had been something of a nine days' wonder after his disappearance in the blizzard, but the fuss had calmed down now. Everything was back to normal.

Rob usually had a lie-in on Saturday mornings. But today Nick had rudely disturbed him from a sound sleep by yanking off the covers and thumping him with a pillow.

'Get up, you lazy slob! Do you want to come scrambling?'

Rob wondered if he'd heard right. Last weekend he'd been allowed a couple of rides on one of the big bikes when his brothers had them out round the fields. Just short rides, because the ground was still wet enough to be damaged by motorbike tyres. But at least he'd been included. Now Peter was doing a weekend job and the ground was drier. It would be just him and Nick.

He blinked up at his brother. 'You mean proper scrambling?'

"Course. I'll take Pete's bike, you can have the Kawasaki. We might go right up to the Bluff.'

Rob needed no second bidding. Already his feet were on the floor and his head in the clothes cupboard, searching for his Motocross gear.

Even Mum did not object, beyond a brief, 'Be careful, now!' as she emerged from the dining-room which she was painting a sickly (Rob thought) shade of pale yellow.

An exhilarating sense of power and freedom filled him as he followed Nick across the farmyard and up the near pasture towards the steep banky field. The air was keen and fresh, the fields greening, the big powerful bike under him revved and throbbed with the promise of carefully controlled power. The lambs were all safely born now. They were in the attractive and inquisitive stage of frisking and leaping and running races in little groups. Their mothers already looked rather weary and careworn, keeping an eye on their offspring as the two bikes roared past.

Rob followed Nick's lead as they rode into the sunken lane, going carefully through the gears, remembering the instructions he had been given, hoping he wouldn't make a fool of himself by stalling the bike, or, even worse, crashing it or falling off. Mum might put her foot down again if he hurt himself, and, even more to be feared, Nick would be livid if he damaged the bike. But so far so good. He was riding the big Kawasaki at last, and he was coping.

The long ridge of the Bluff loomed above them, purplish blue and hazy, its whinberry- and heather-covered slopes offering perfect scrambling tracks. Rob wondered how far Nick would take him, but didn't ask. Best just to follow on and not push his luck.

They rode steadily at a moderate pace until suddenly they had topped a rise and were looking down at a place that seemed strangely familiar. There was a little huddle of grey stone farm buildings tucked away in a fold under the mountains, and surrounded by rowans, hawthorn and stunted fruit trees. It had been covered and half-buried in whiteness when he'd last seen it. Ty Mynydd.

They paused for a moment on the ridge, idling the engines, looking down at Amos' place. A thin plume of blue smoke rose from the chimney. White dots of sheep and lambs showed on the smooth grassy plateau where the helicopter had landed. They'd heard no news of Amos since the blizzard. Had Megan arrived as planned? How was Amos managing?

Suddenly Rob wanted very much to know. He turned to Nick. 'Could we go down for a minute and see Amos?'

For a moment he thought Nick might refuse. He liked to be the one giving the orders and calling the shots. Then Nick said, 'OK then. Let's go.'

A battered truck stood not far from the porch door. Amos himself appeared at the door as they rode into the farmyard, past the lambing shed, now empty, and the barking chorus of young dogs. Rob pushed up his helmet visor and grinned.

'Hello, Amos.'

The old man's face split into an answering grin. 'Well, if it bain't young Roberts, Penvaen. And his brother, I see. Well, indeed! Come on in. Have a cup of tea.'

They dismounted and followed the old man inside. Rob's arms and legs were aching and wobbly, and he felt he'd be glad of a bit of a rest. Those big bikes took more managing than he'd realized, though he'd never admit it to anyone, especially Nick.

Inside, he could hardly believe the transformation. Gone was the smelly sheep-pen in the corner and in its place stood a shiny new calor-gas cooker. The floor was scrubbed and clean, windows shining, clutter tidied away and table tops spotless. A pot of bright yellow chrysanthemums stood on the window-sill. Amos' bed was still there against one wall, but it was neatly made and covered by a bright woven cover. Plump cushions sat in the armchairs. The only familiar thing seemed to be Floss, who had retained her place in front of the fire and looked up at Rob with a thump of her tail as he entered.

'Did Megan come, then?' asked Rob.

Amos was putting a kettle on the shining new cooker. 'Aye. Her came. Stayed three weeks, and put me to rights.' He chuckled, well pleased with himself and the transformation of his home. He looked well, and moved about quite easily. With his old knack of seeming to read Rob's thoughts, he said, 'I'm a lot better than I was. Much sharper. The doctor's changed me tablets. Wonderful what they can do these days, it is.'

'And what about the sheep? Did you manage the lambing okay?'

'Oh aye. Had plenty of help. Megan brought Brad along, you see. Me youngest grandson. He's still here, staying on for a bit to study up on hill farming.'

The old man was setting out mugs, getting out milk and sugar and biscuits. Proper milk, Rob noticed, not powdered—and a little gas fridge to keep it fresh.

There was a scrape of boots in the porch and a tall young man came in, as tall as Nick, with keen blue eyes and a deep tan. Amos introduced him as Brad, and the two young men shook hands, looking each other squarely in the eye. Rob thought that Nick and Brad looked quite alike, tall and straight and muscular. Maybe it was because of the Air Force training they'd both had. Brad also looked a bit like one of the stars of Rob's favourite Australian soap, and sounded rather like him too when he spoke.

'Good day. So you're the Roberts brothers. Grandad's told me all about you. Where are you stationed now, Nick?'

The two of them hit it off straight away. They pulled up two kitchen chairs and soon Brad and Nick were deep in Air Force talk as they drank their tea.

Amos gave Rob a nudge. 'Take a look round the rest of the house. Brad's got it all sorted out. Heaters in all the bedrooms, and all the damp dried out. We're connected up to the electric now. Even a telly. I never thought I'd take to that, but I quite likes the wildlife programmes, and the news, and the travel programmes. A real eye-opener, it is.'

He sat down in his favourite armchair, mug in hand, half-listening to the conversation of the two young men, well pleased with himself and with life in general. Rob wandered upstairs to look at the newly-occupied rooms with their neatly-made beds, then down again and through into the little front parlour. Here, too, everything was dusted and polished, the faded carpet swept, kindling and logs in the fireplace ready to be lit and a brand new TV set in the corner beside it.

Rob stood in the middle of the room, remembering the days and nights he'd spent here marooned on this little farm with a vast sea of snow outside. It seemed a very long time ago, though it wasn't really all that long. Only a month. The dreams he'd had on the first lonely, homesick night came into his mind. He'd told no one about them, not even Mum. There was no way he could explain the vividness and reality of them, the colour and movement, the way he somehow knew what it was like to be Rac, and cared so much about Bara. Rob wished he knew whether they'd been real people and what had happened to them. But it was something he could never know.

He sighed, standing in the middle of the room.

Amos' creaky voice called through from the kitchen. 'You can put a match to that fire, my lad, if you likes. That there Australian play comes on soon, and we might as well watch it in comfort. We got enough stew to go round if you wants to stay to dinner.'

Rob picked up the box of matches from the mantlepiece. Amos was obviously set on prolonging their visit. They'd brought sandwiches with them, and Rob had hoped that he and Nick would spend the whole day together. He sighed again and put a match to the kindling in the grate.

The paper and dry wood caught and blazed up, licking around the small logs in the fireplace. A basket full of chopped wood stood beside the hearth, ready to feed the fire. Brad was obviously well organized in every way. The flames crackled and leapt, beginning to take the chill off the little room. Rob knelt in front of the fire and held out his chilly hands to the blaze.

The hearthstone was one single large slab of the grey mountain granite, and on the surface of the stone something was carved, beginning to show clearly in the light of the dancing flames. Rob held his breath suddenly, leaning forward on hands and knees to peer more closely at it.

Old marks on stone, carved and chiselled deeply and lovingly, worn a little with the passing of the centuries, but still clear in their detail. A young woman with long hair and a gentle smile, a necklace of teeth about her neck and bone ornaments in her ears. In her arms she held a fat baby and at her elbow stood a girl almost as tall as herself. A small boy stood at her knees. And there were sheep. Strange-looking sheep, long-coated and curly-horned, but unmistakably sheep, a flock of them, taking up almost all the space on the slab of stone.

'Bara,' said Rob softly.

He sat back on his heels in the flickering firelight, feeling somehow complete. He felt suddenly deeply grateful—to be alive, to be here with Nick, to see old Amos again. He thought back to the blizzard. He might not have survived, if it hadn't been for Amos. He thought of Amos, his face grey with pain, lying as if dead out there in the yard. He thought about how he had desperately called to God to help him...

A sense of peace filled him, and filled the room. And there was something else too—a Presence that was all-loving and all-powerful and spanned the ages between himself and Rac and Bara as though they were no more than a day. Amos' words came back to him, words of Jesus: 'I am the good shepherd, and I know my sheep...'

'Switch on the telly,' called Amos from the next room. 'Give it a chance to warm up before the programme.'

'It doesn't need to warm up, Grandad,' said Brad.

'All machines needs warming up,' insisted Amos. 'That's the nature of 'em.'

Rob didn't move for a moment. He didn't really want to watch a television programme, or talk, or do anything that would disturb the sense of peace that filled him. He was reluctant to join the others, loath to lose this moment of realization that would be a milestone in his life. He wished they could just take off, him and Nick, climbing up into the mountains with the wind on their faces and nothing but the sky over their heads and the rest of the day in front of them.

He was afraid, though, that their plans would now be changed. Nick and Brad were chatting like old friends, mates who had known each other for ages. Already they had fixed up a date for Tuesday night, to play snooker at the Community Hall.

'I wouldn't mind a go on those bikes, either,' said Brad. 'Done a bit of scrambling myself down under. Would you lend me a bike?'

'Sure,' said Nick. Rob felt his heart sink. He knew that Nick was going to offer Brad the Kawasaki, now, today. There were only two bikes, which meant he'd probably be parked here with Amos while they were away.

Tears pricked behind his eyes. But Nick was speaking again, pushing back his chair with a scrape on the kitchen floor. 'We'll fix up something with the bikes, middle of the week maybe, okay? Can't today. Me and my brother are off up to the Bluff. We've brought sandwiches so I'm afraid we'll say no thanks to lunch, Amos. Thanks for the tea and the chat, though.' He raised his voice. 'Hey, Rob, what are you doing in there? Time we were on our way!'

Rob took one more look at the stone carvings that had survived the passing of the centuries. Then he was on his feet, going out into the next room, saying his goodbyes before he followed his brother out into the bright spring morning.

More stories from Lion Publishing for you to enjoy:

THE LITTLE WHITE HORSE Elizabeth Goudge	£3.50 ☐
A WITCH IN TIME William Raeper	£2.99 ☐
WARRIOR OF LIGHT William Raeper	£3.50 ☐
FEAR IN THE GLEN Jenny Robertson	£2.50 ☐
TALES FROM THE ARK Avril Rowlands	£3.50 ☐
DANGER AT DARK HOWS Patricia Sibley	£3.50 ☐
GREYBACK Eleanor Watkins	£2.50 ☐
THE MAGIC IN THE POOL OF MAKING Beth Webb	£2.99 ☐

All Lion paperbacks are available from your local bookshop or newsagent, or can be ordered direct from the address below. Just tick the titles you want and fill in the form.

Name (Block letters) _____

Address _____

_____

Write to Lion Publishing, Cash Sales Department, PO Box 11, Falmouth, Cornwall TR10 9EN, England.

Please enclose a cheque or postal order to the value of the cover price plus:

UK INCLUDING BFPO: £1.00 for the first book, 50p for the second book and 30p for each additional book ordered to a maximum charge of £3.00.

OVERSEAS INCLUDING EIRE: £2.00 for the first book, £1.00 for the second book and 50p for each additional book.

Lion Publishing reserves the right to show on covers and charge new retail prices which may differ from those previously advertised in the text or elsewhere, and to increase postal rates in accordance with the Post Office.